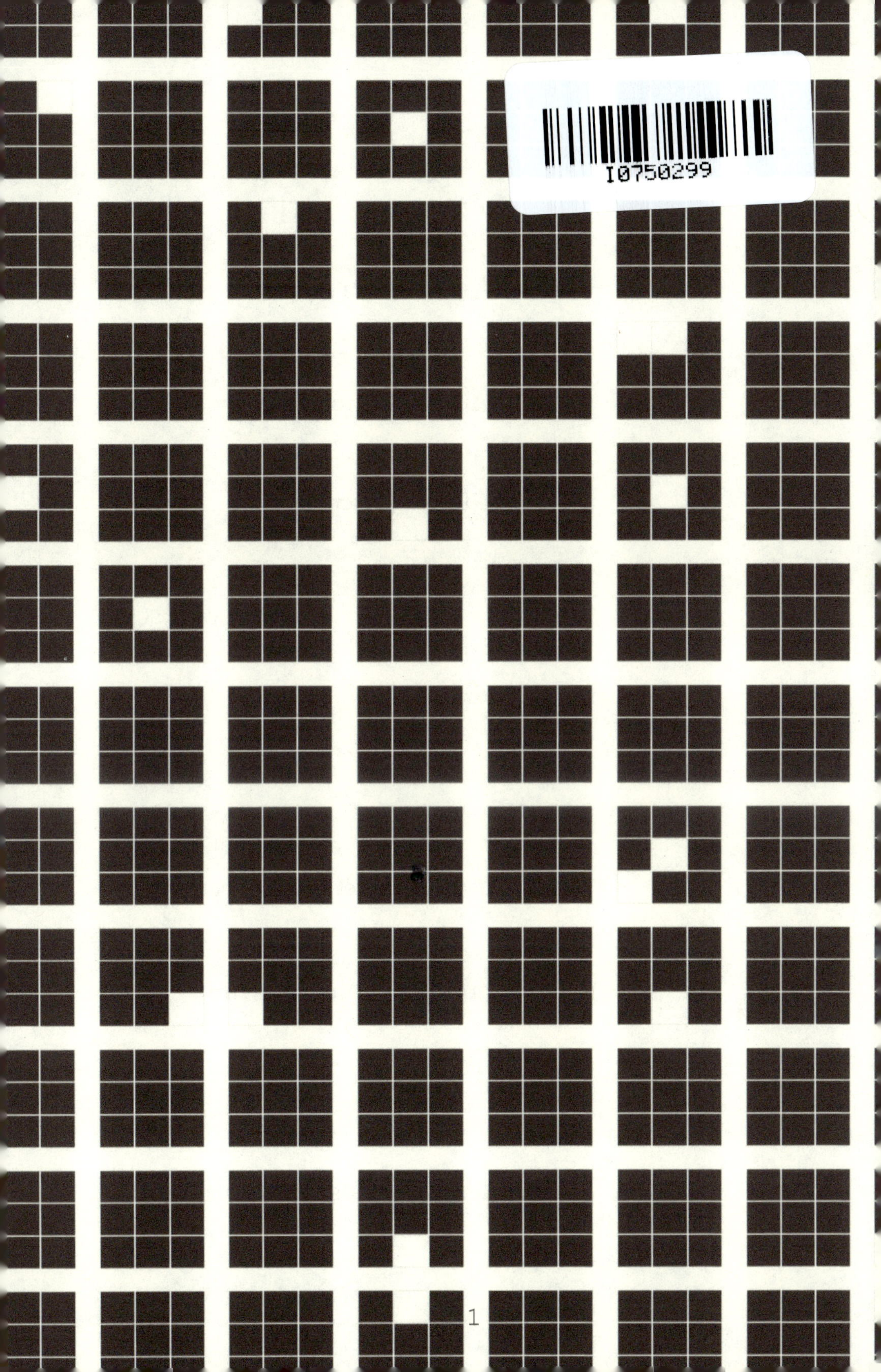
I0750299

Post-Asemic Press 003

ISBN: 978-1-7328788-1-5

Contact: postasemicpress@gmail.com

postasemicpress.blogspot.com

Cover design by Rosaire Appel

z i n c
z a n c
z u n c

an asemic conjugation

by Rosaire Appel

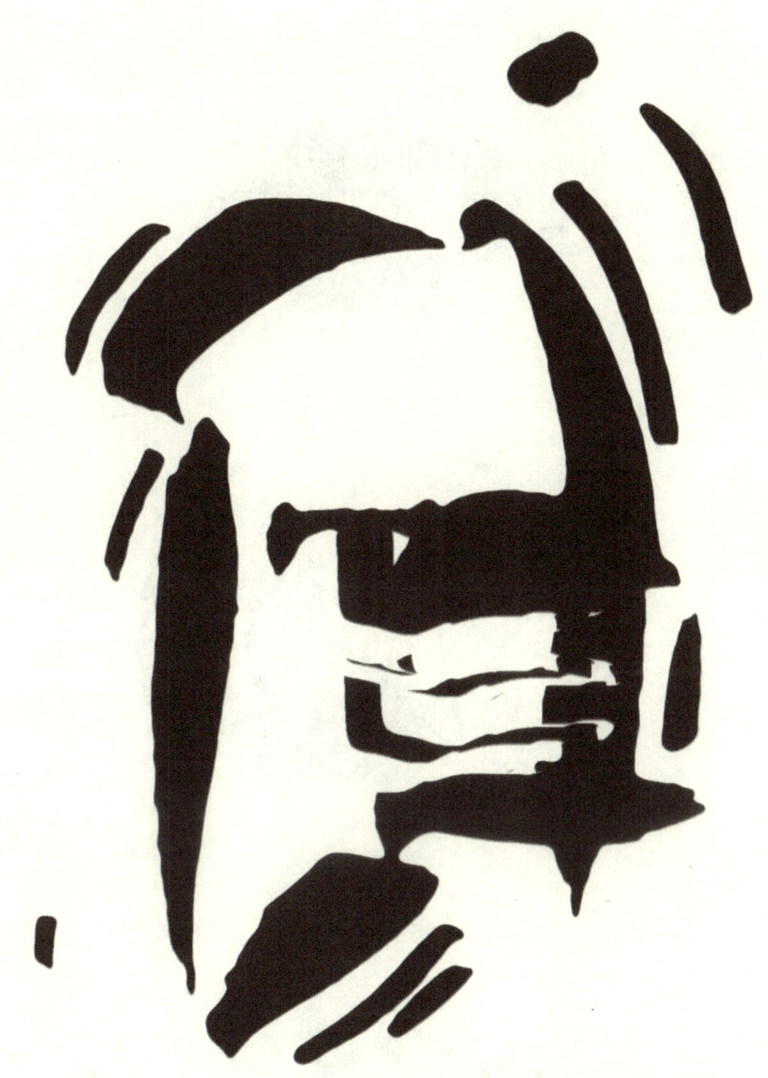

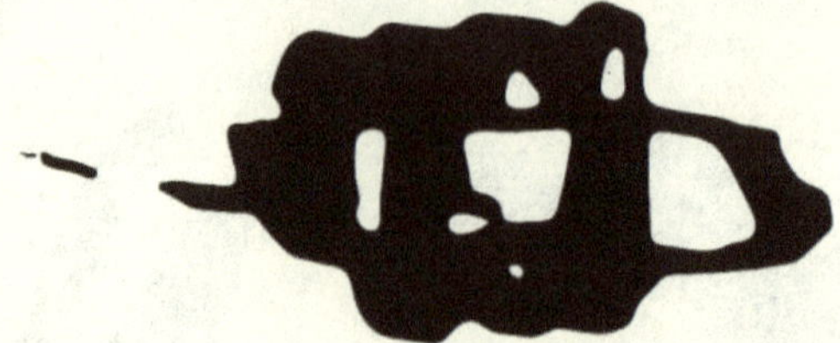

ZINC

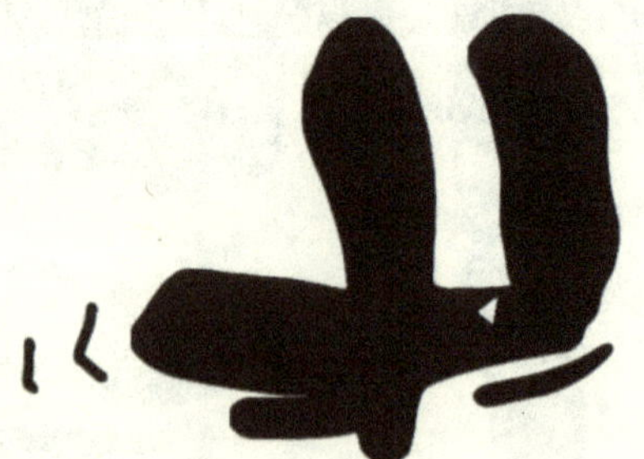

ZANC

ZUNK

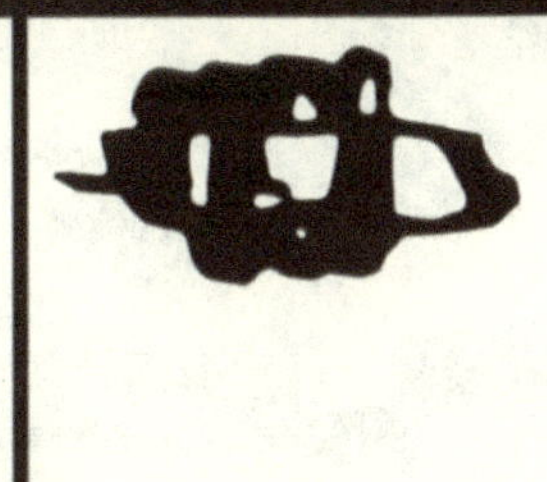

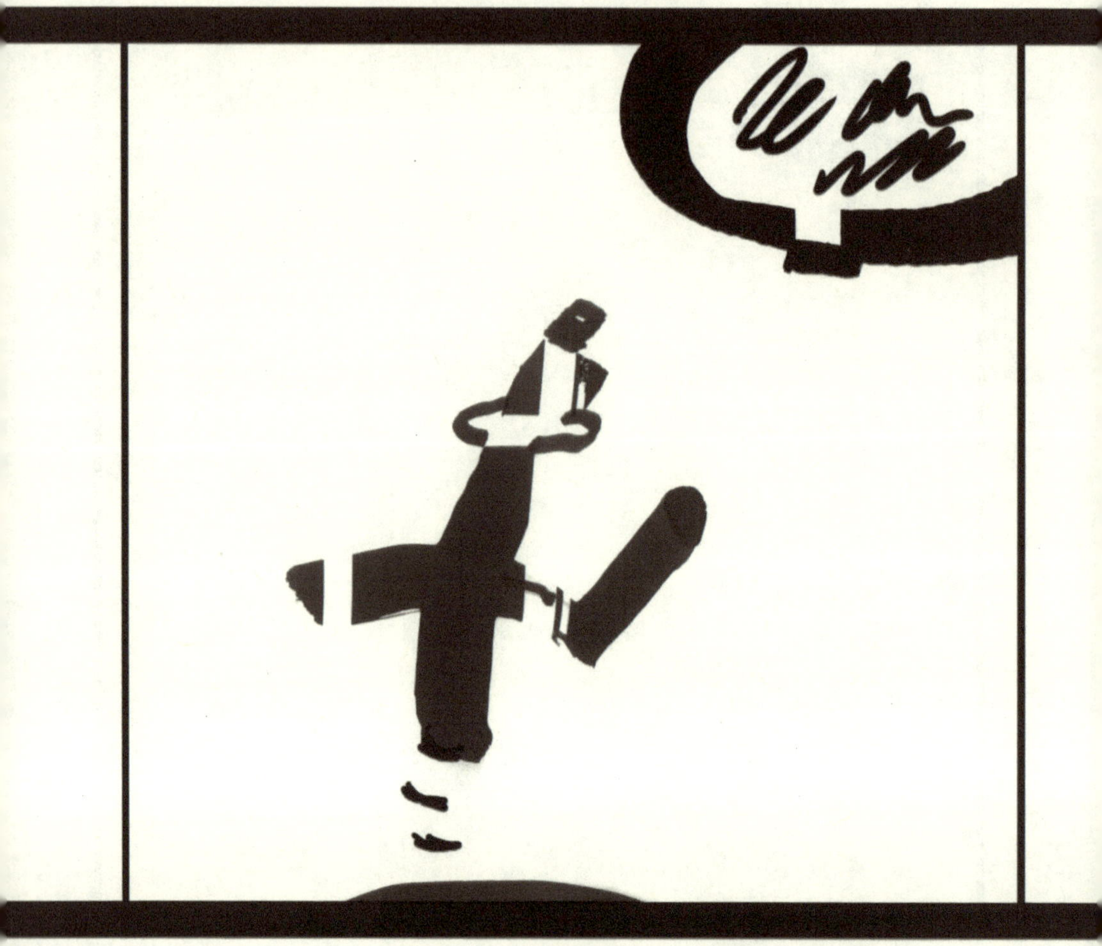

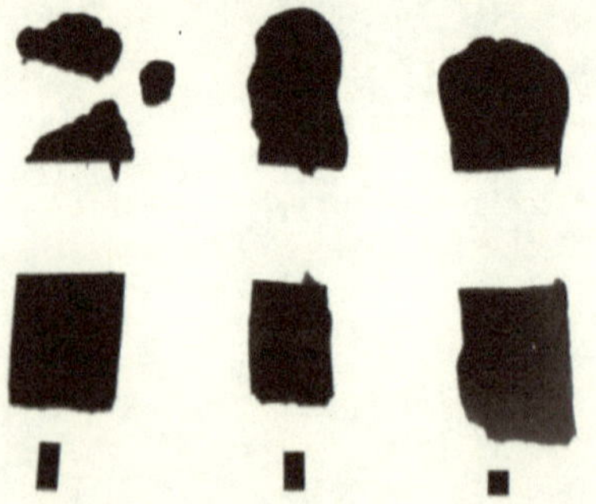

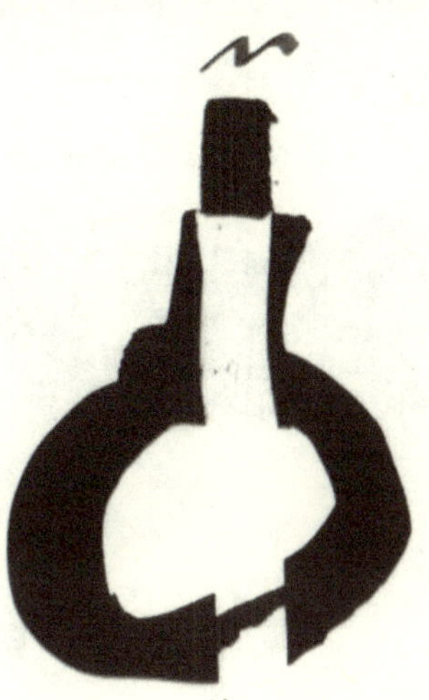

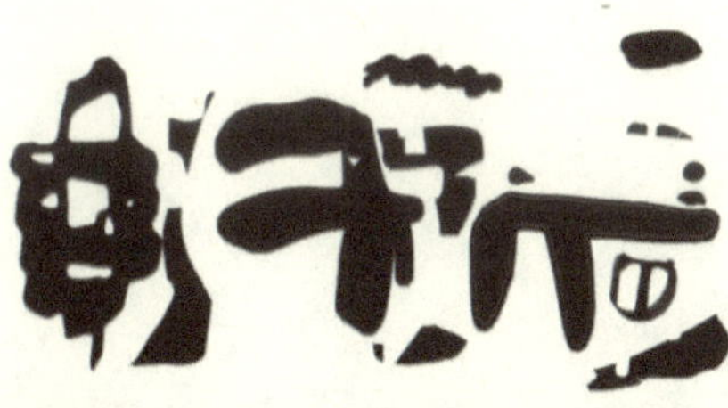

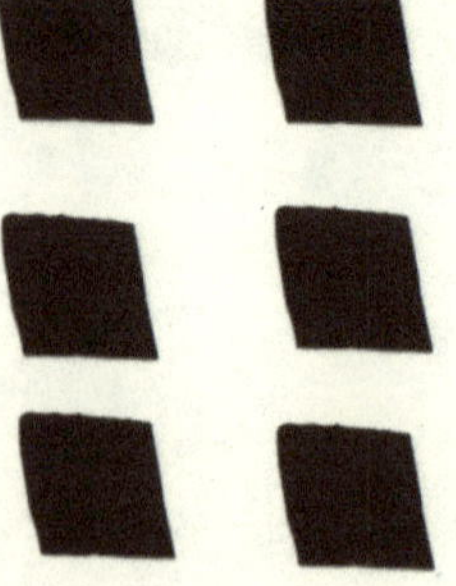

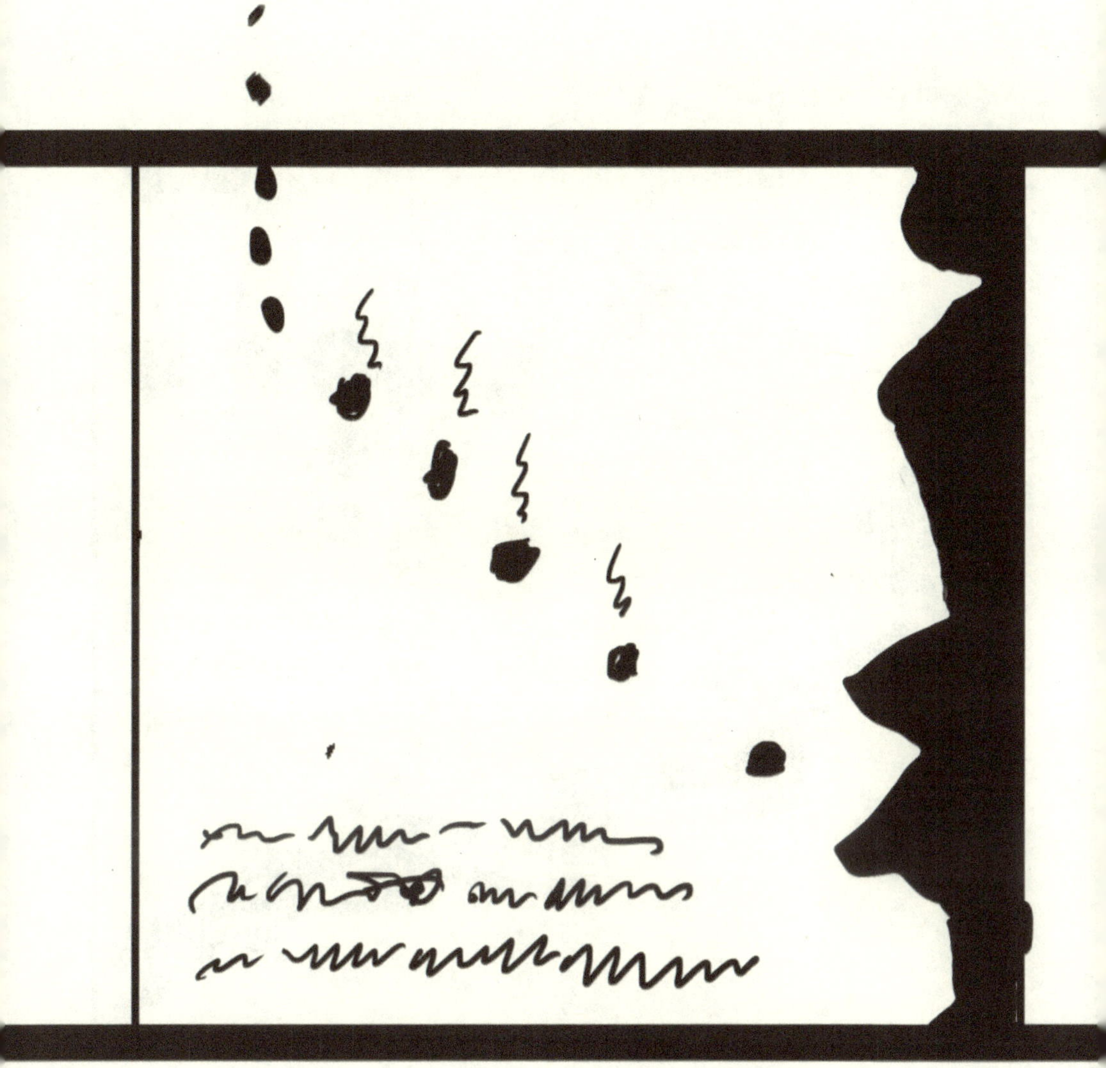

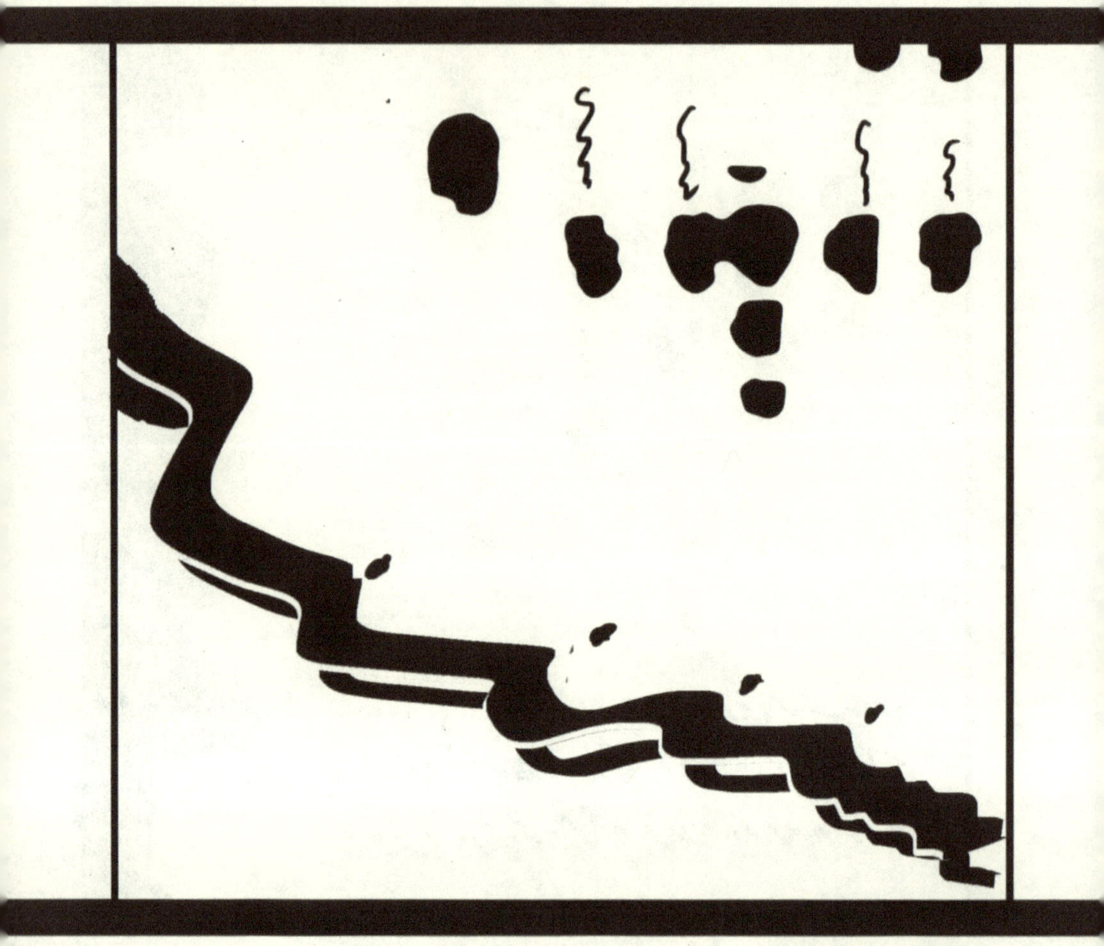

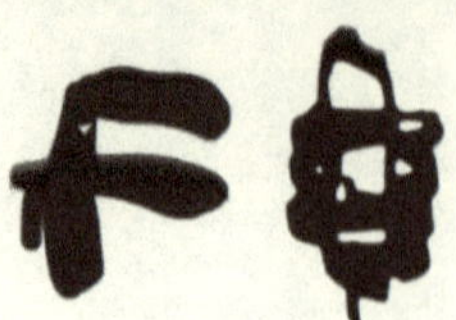

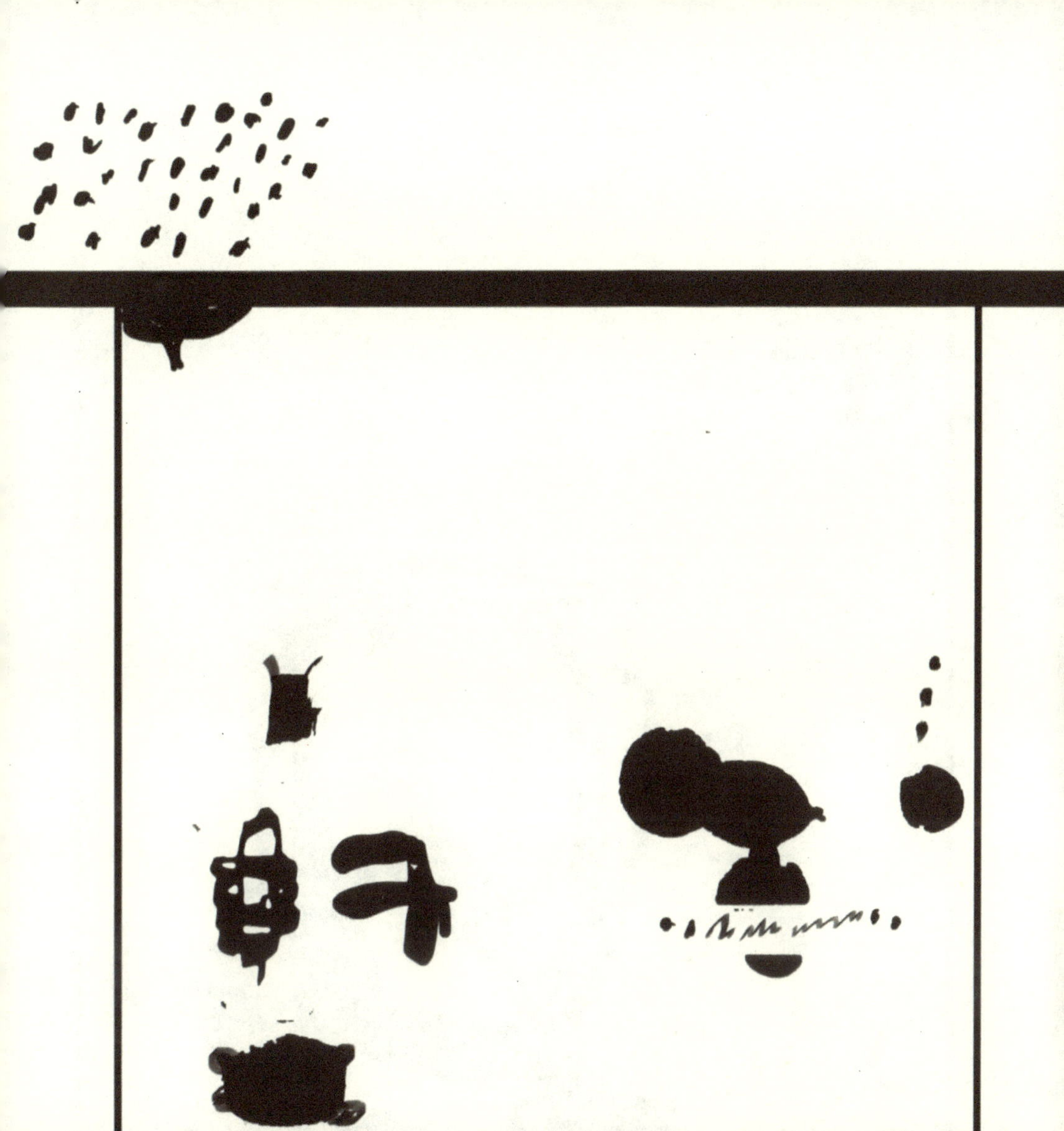

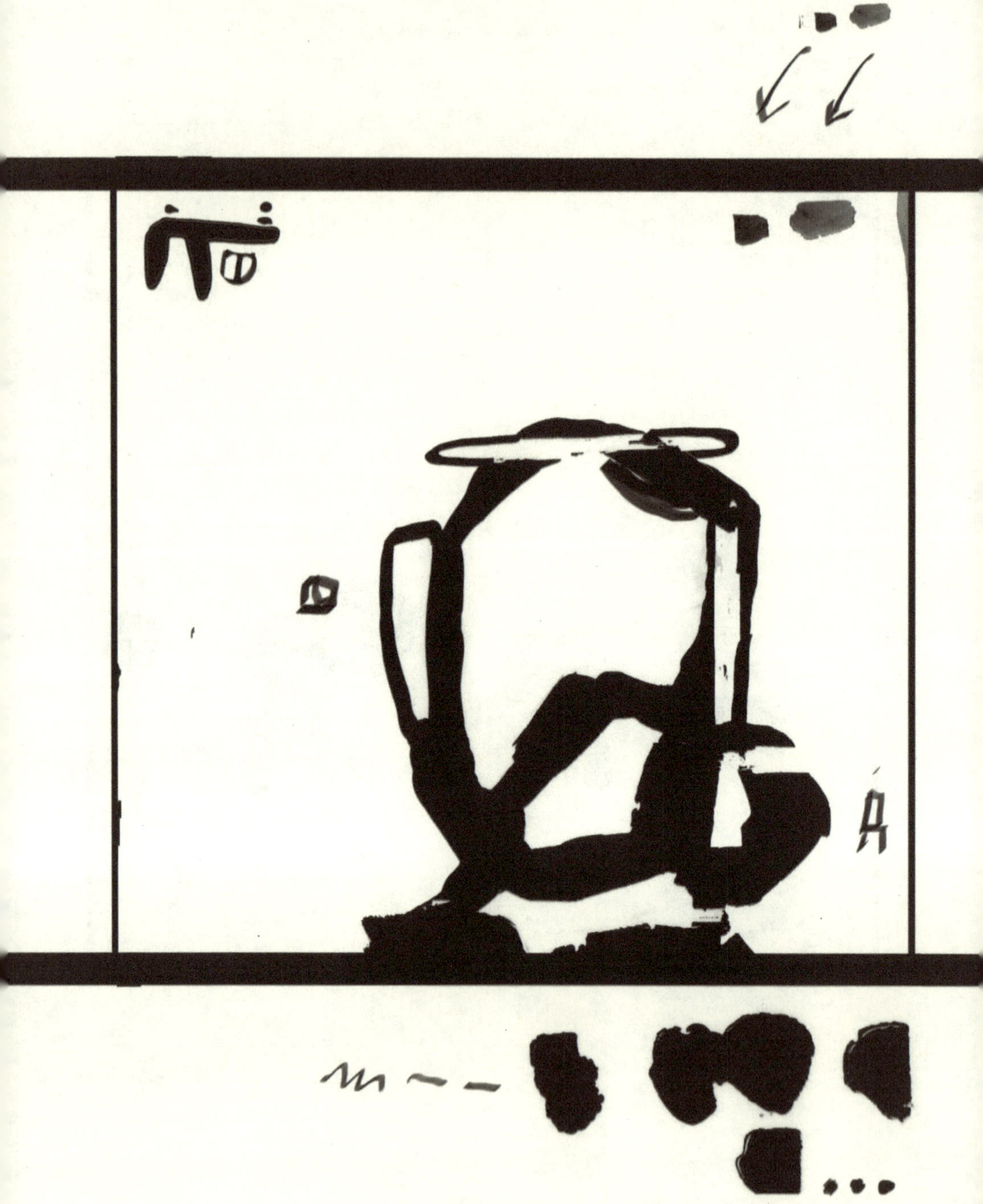

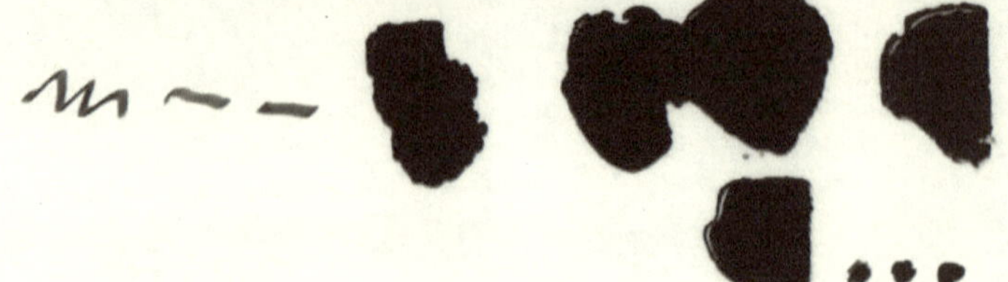

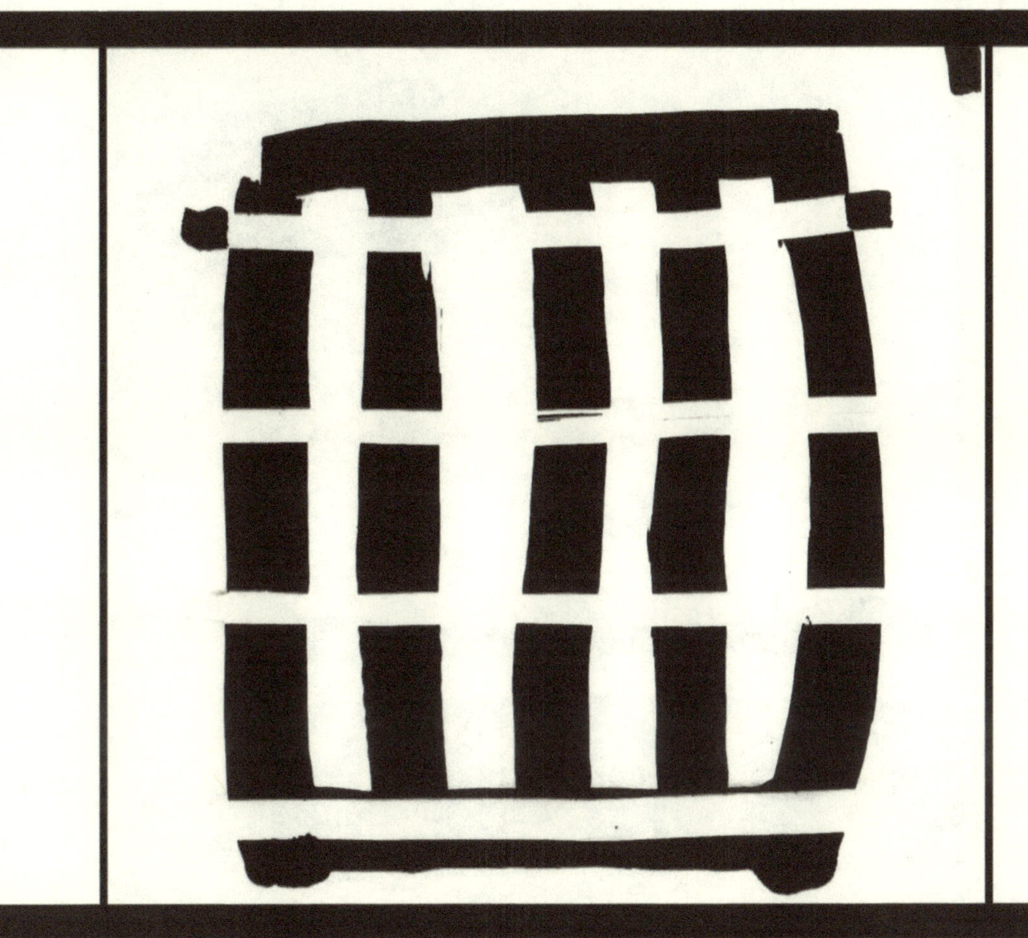

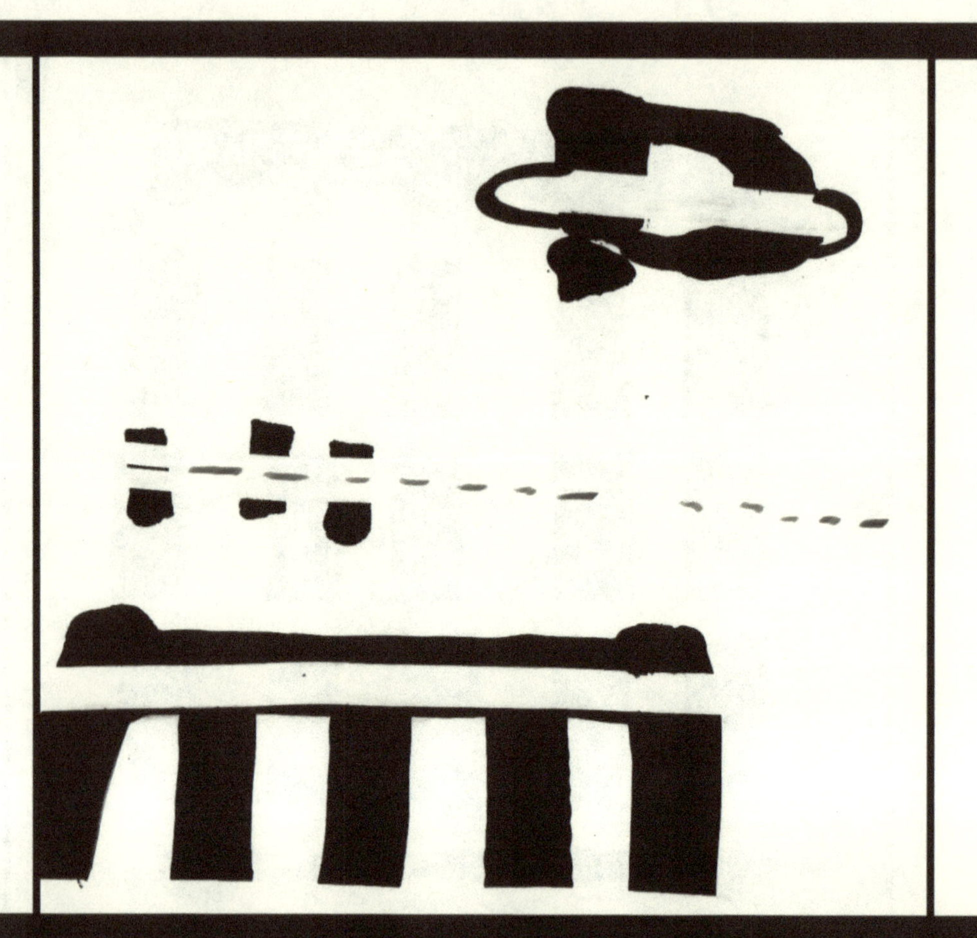

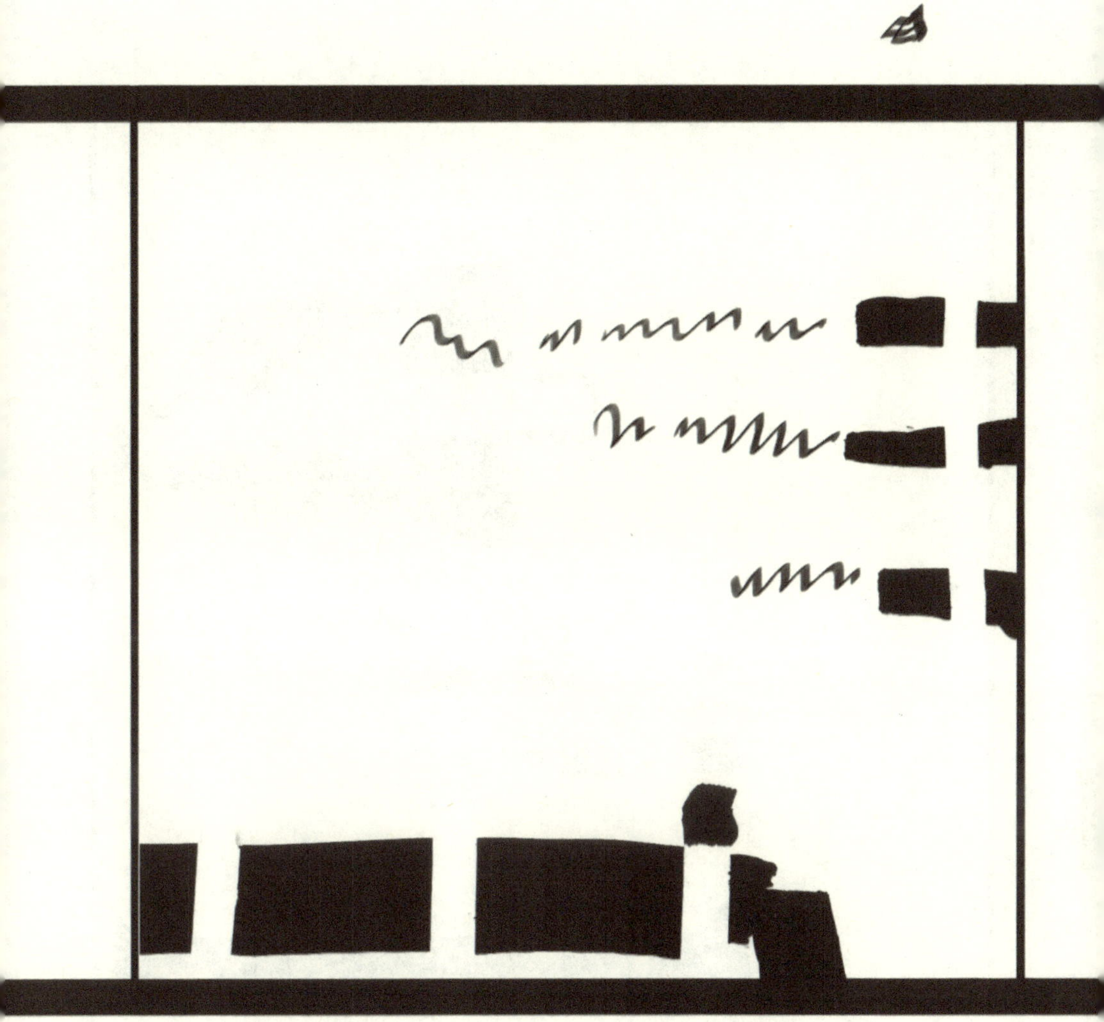

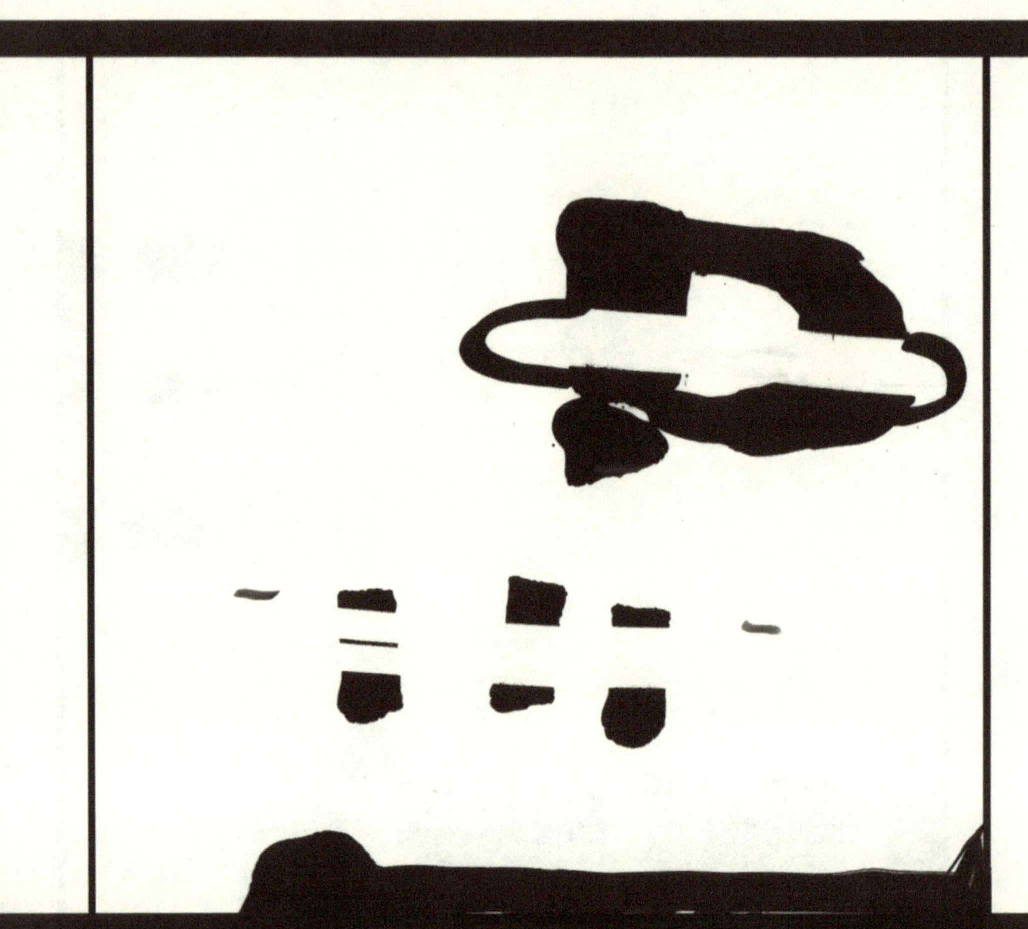

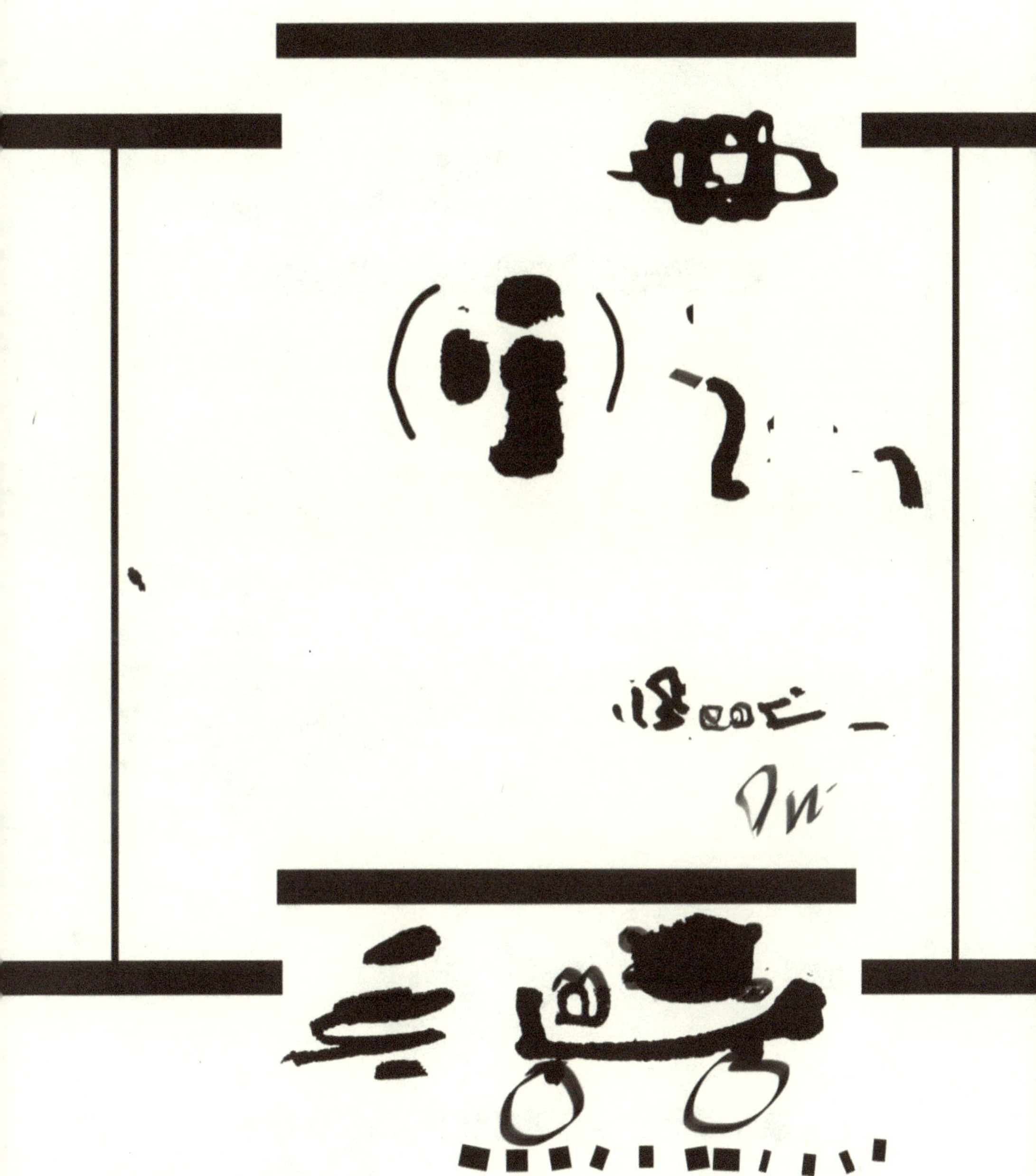

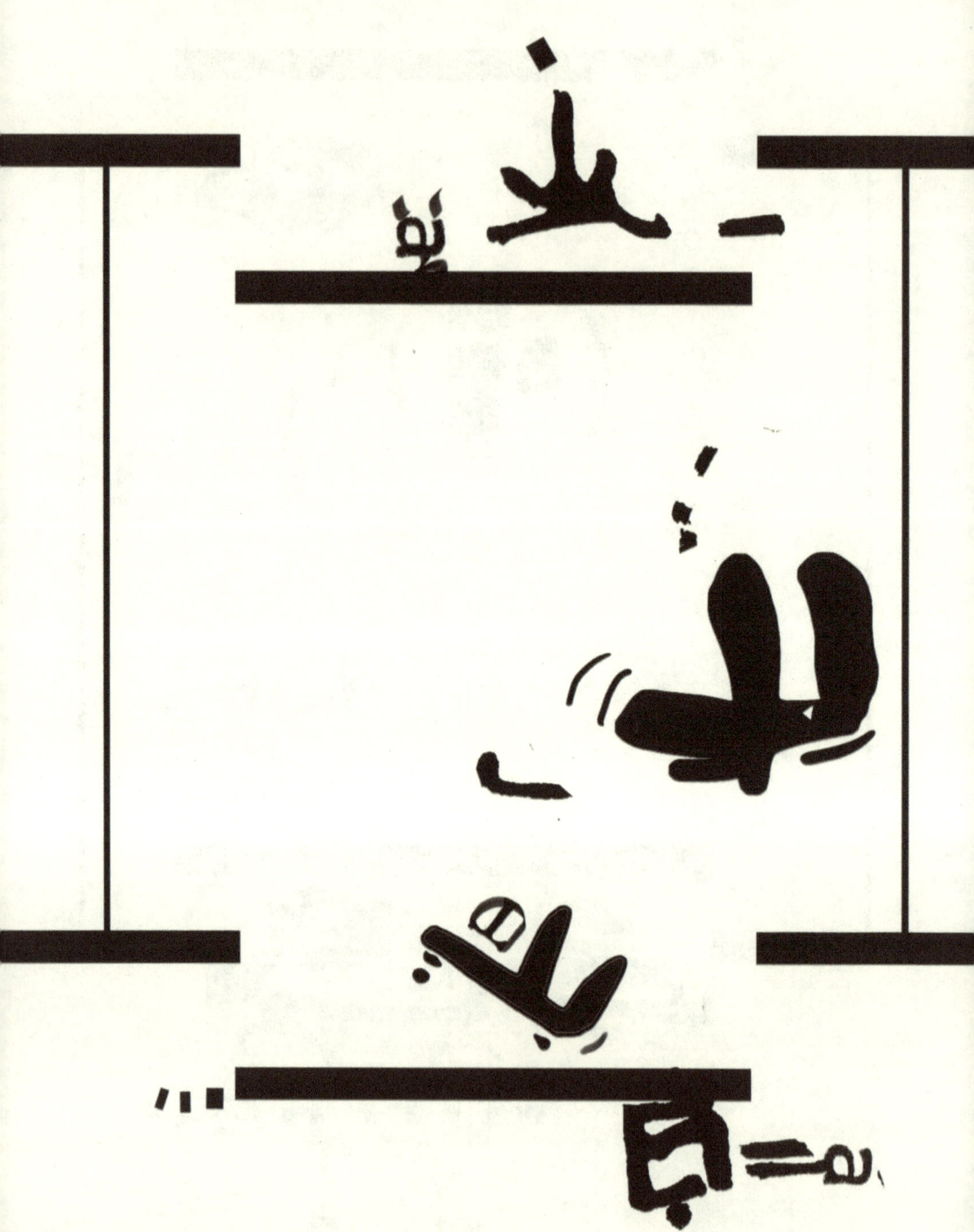

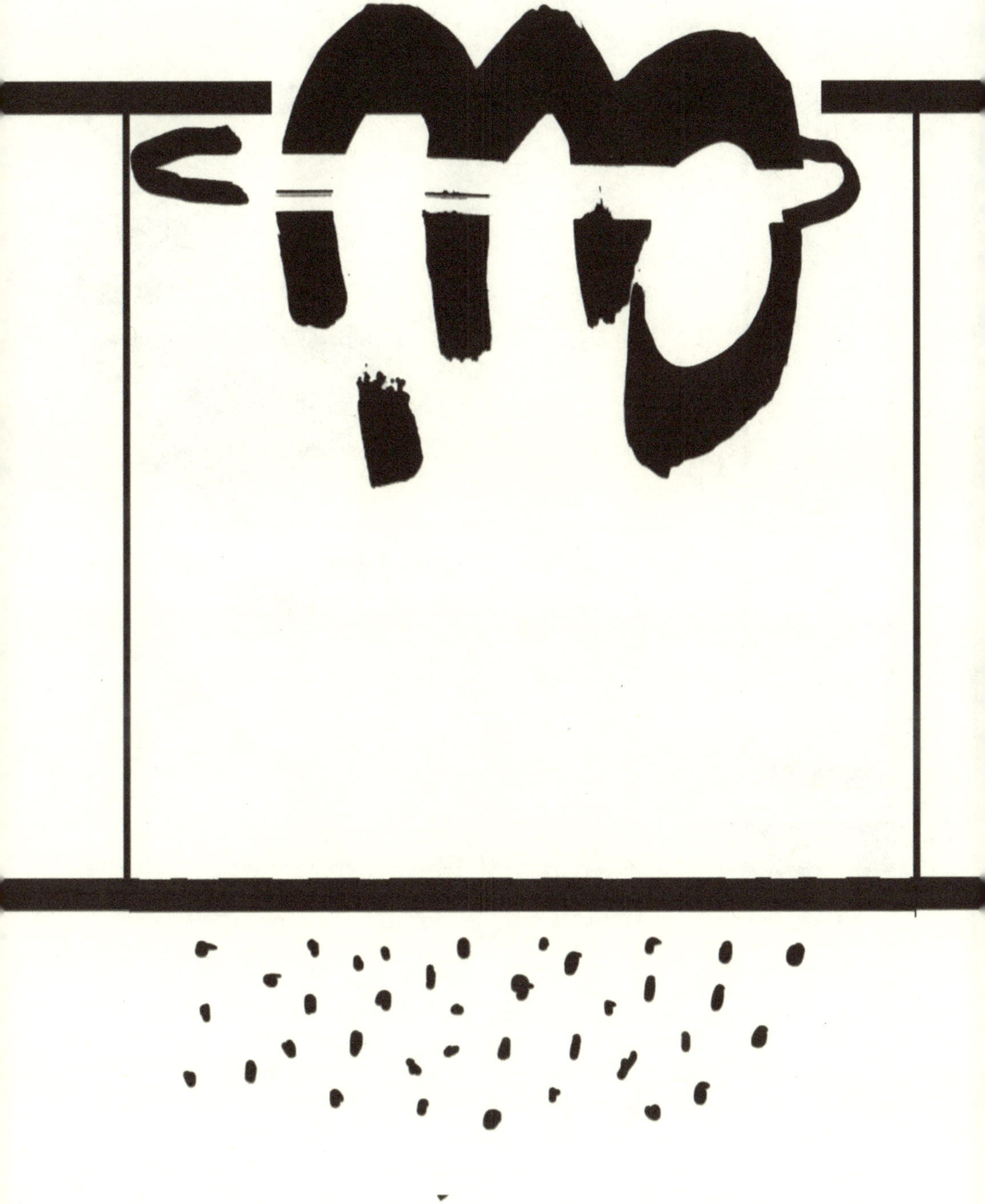

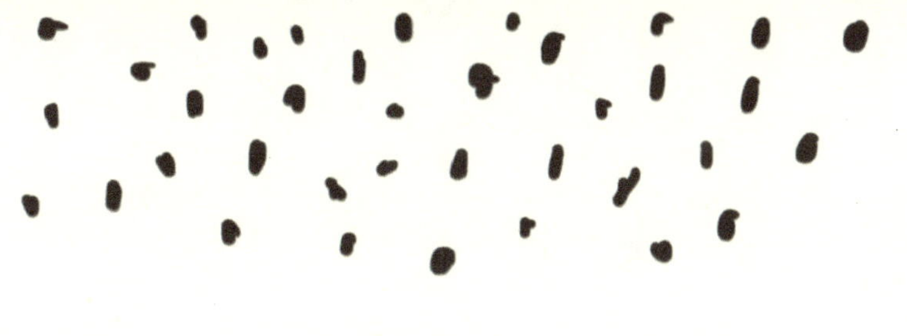

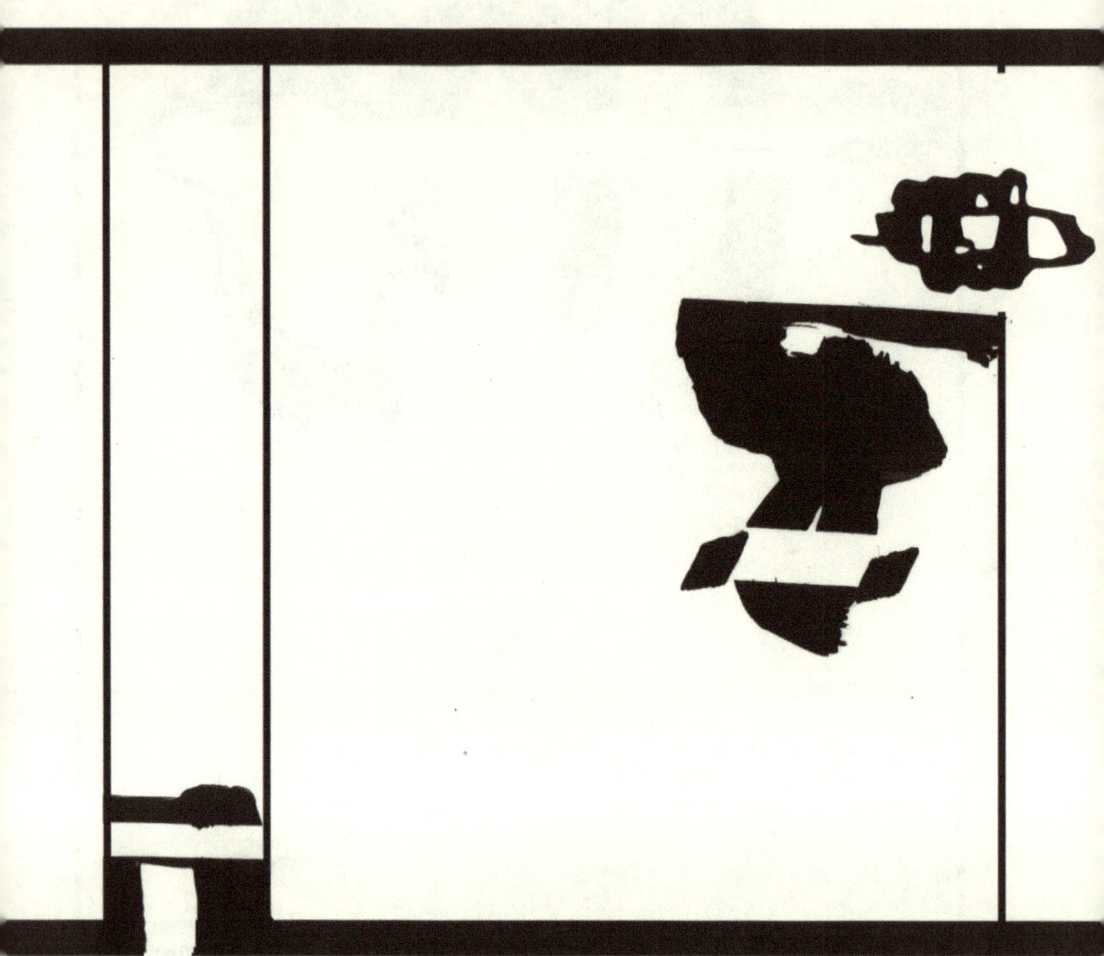

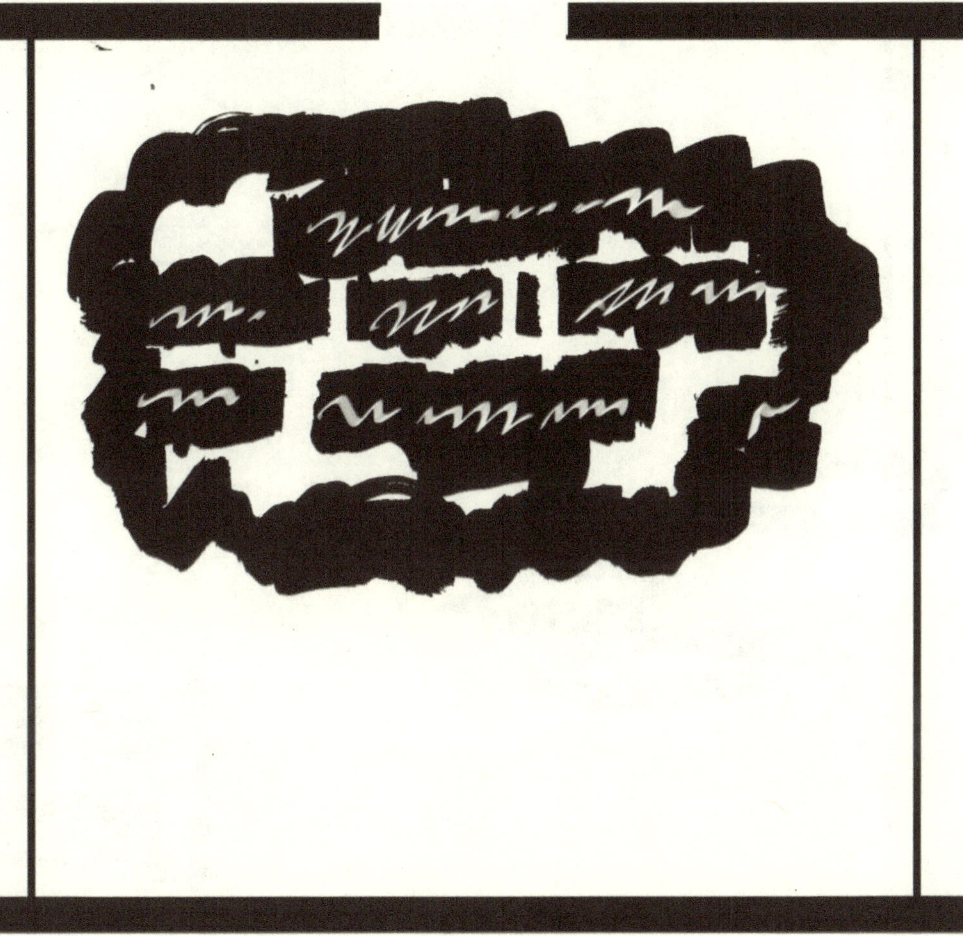

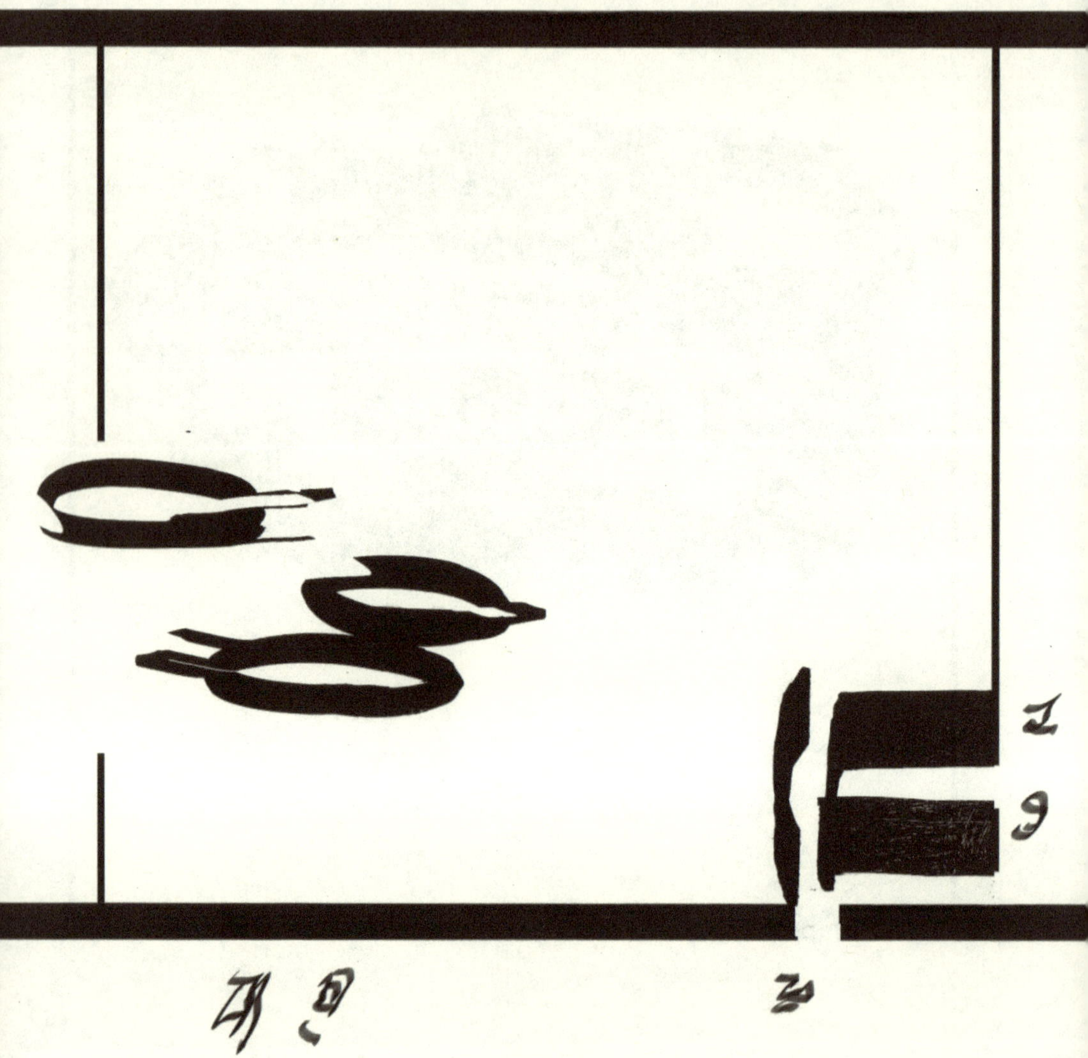

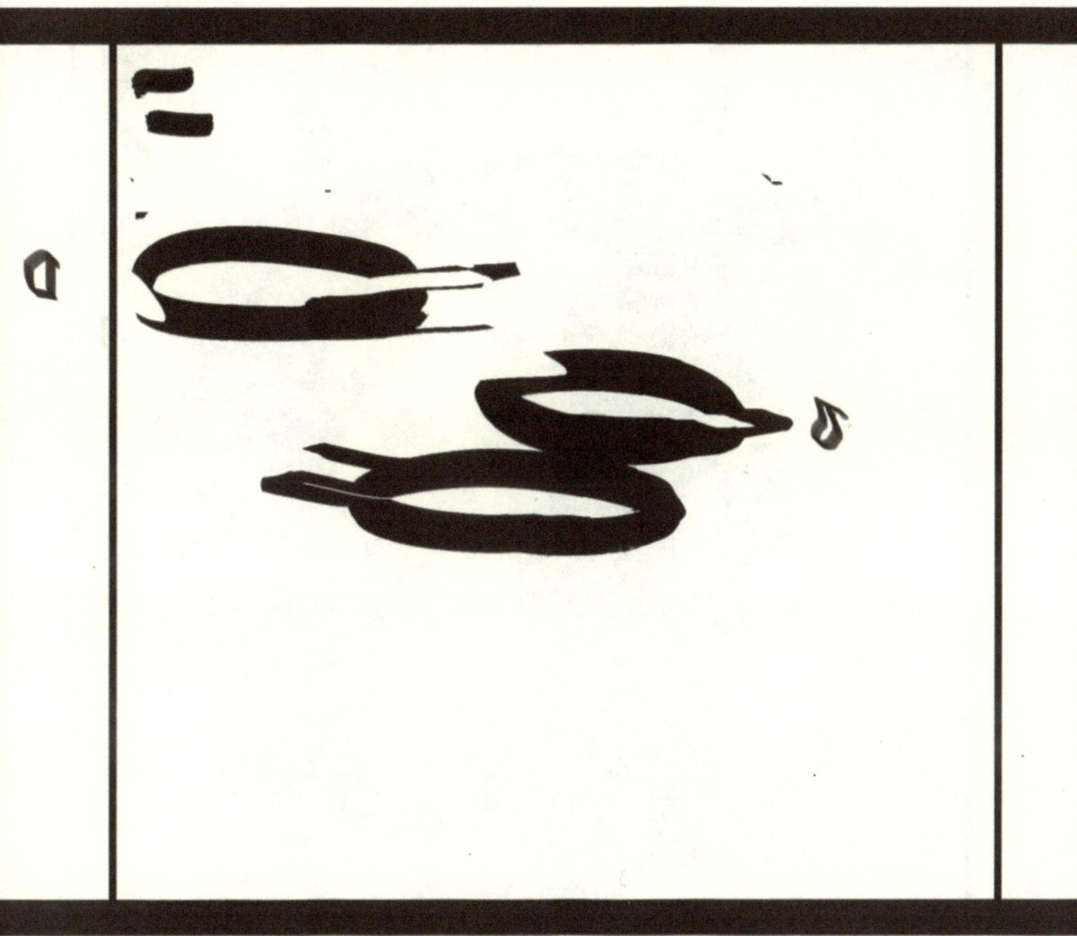

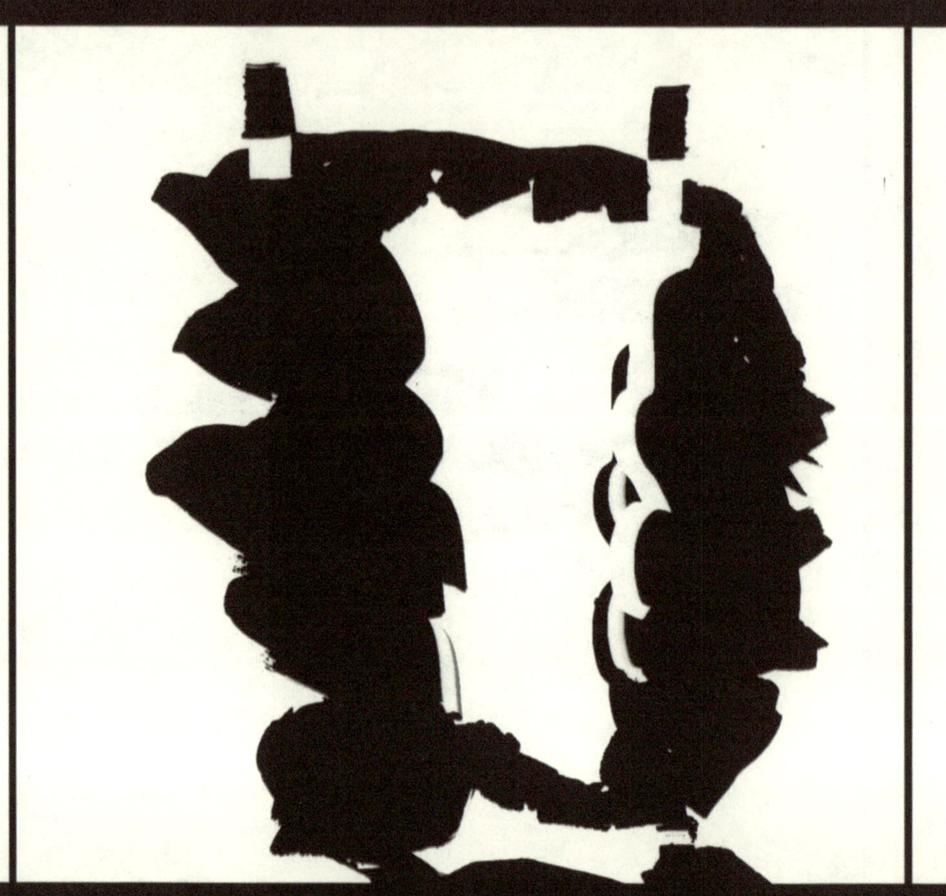

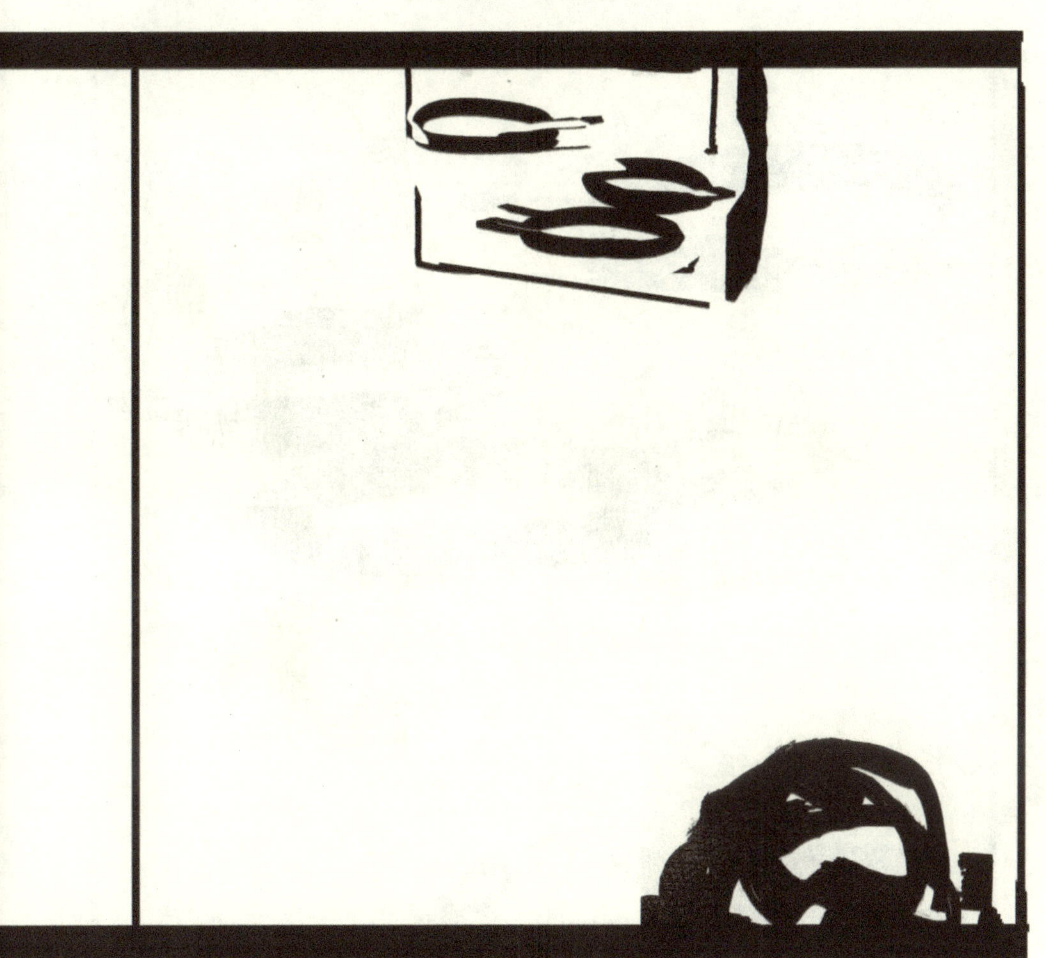

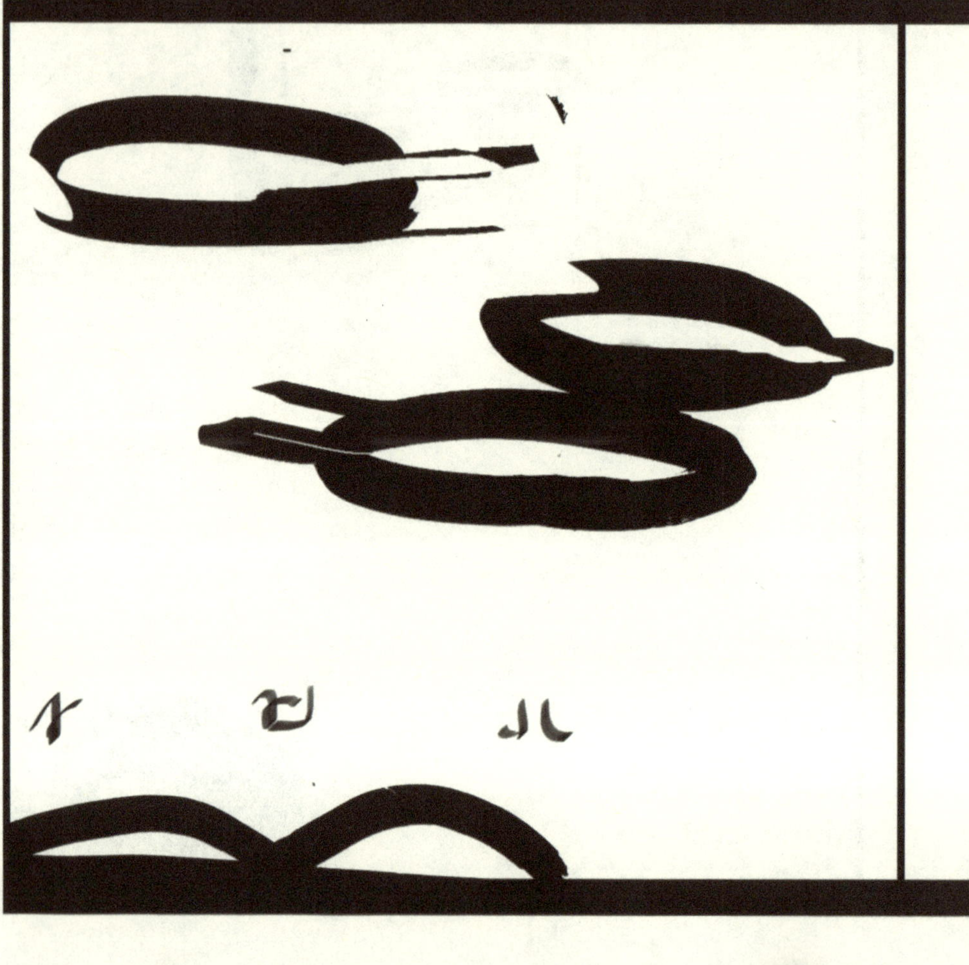

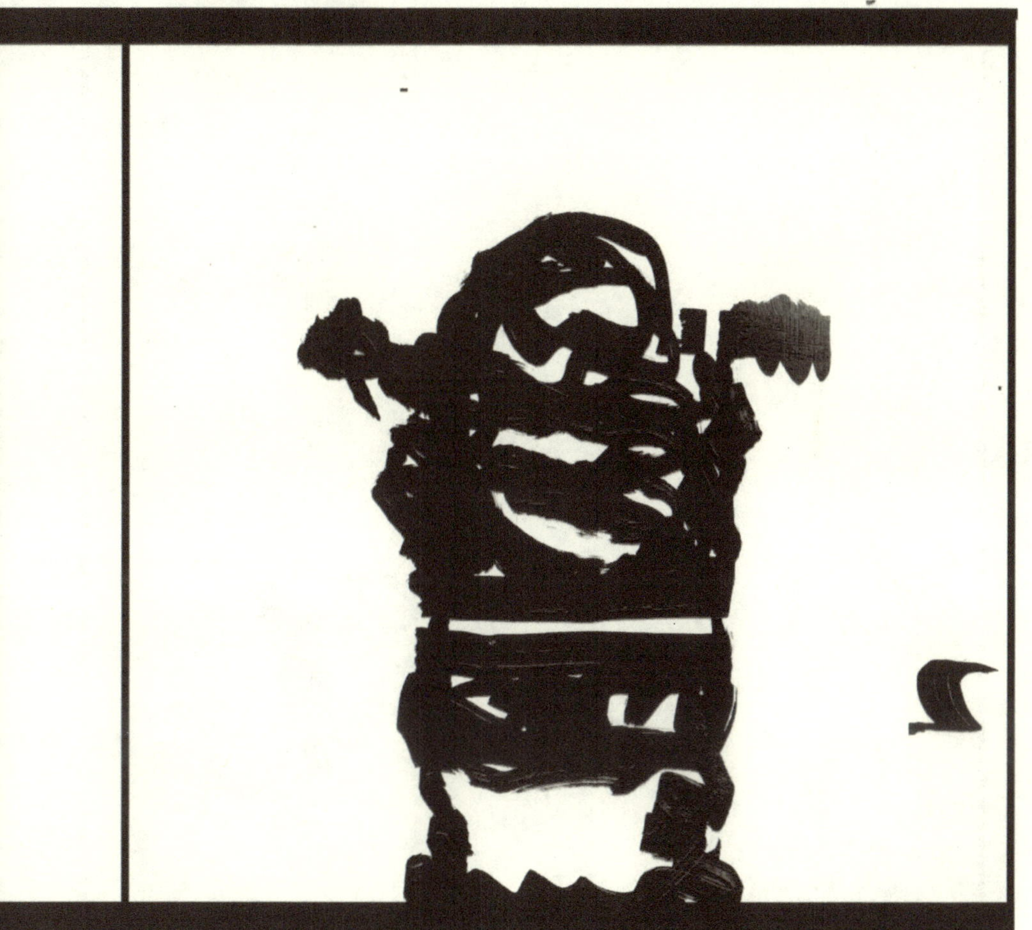

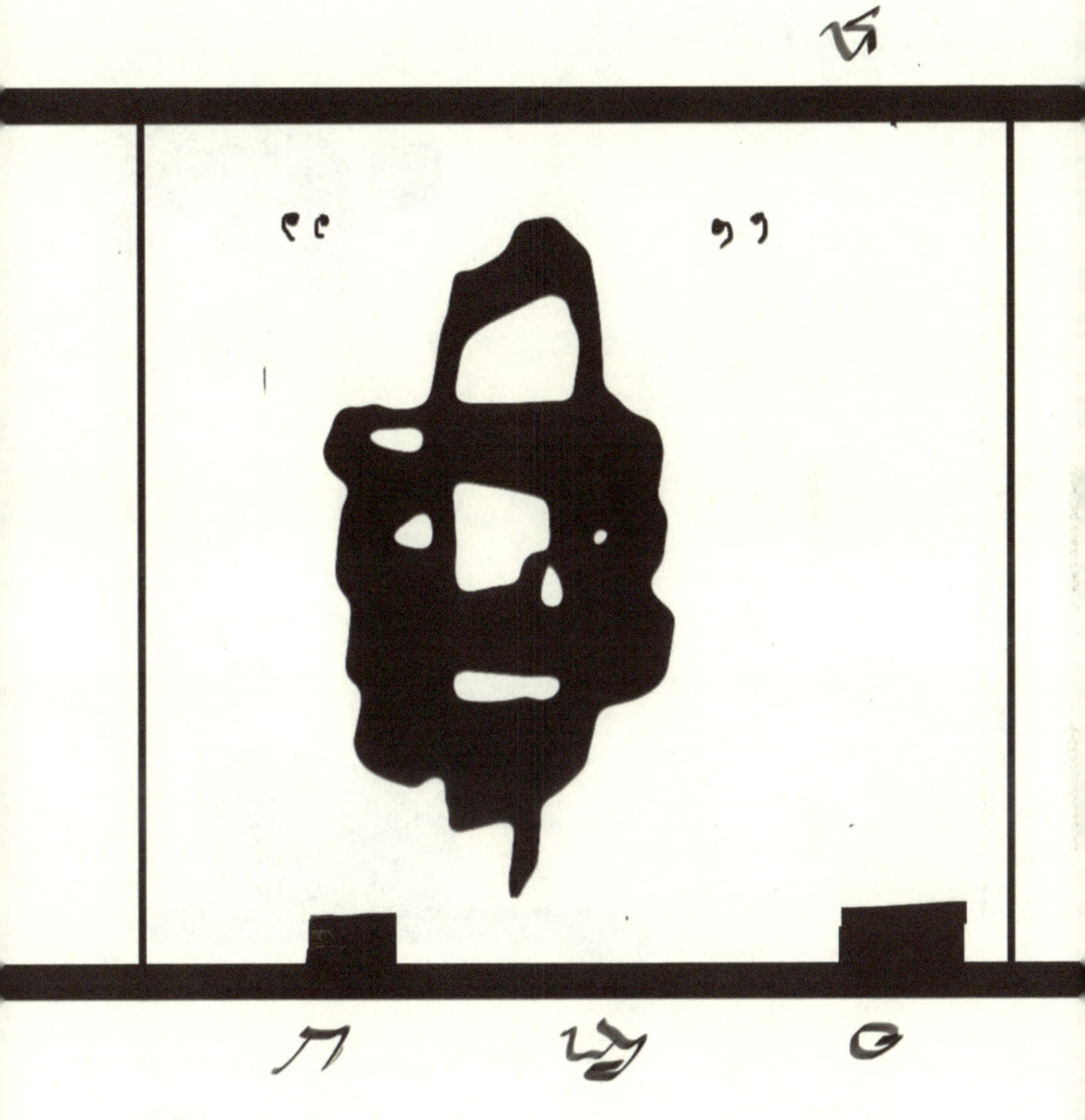

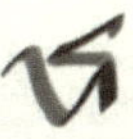

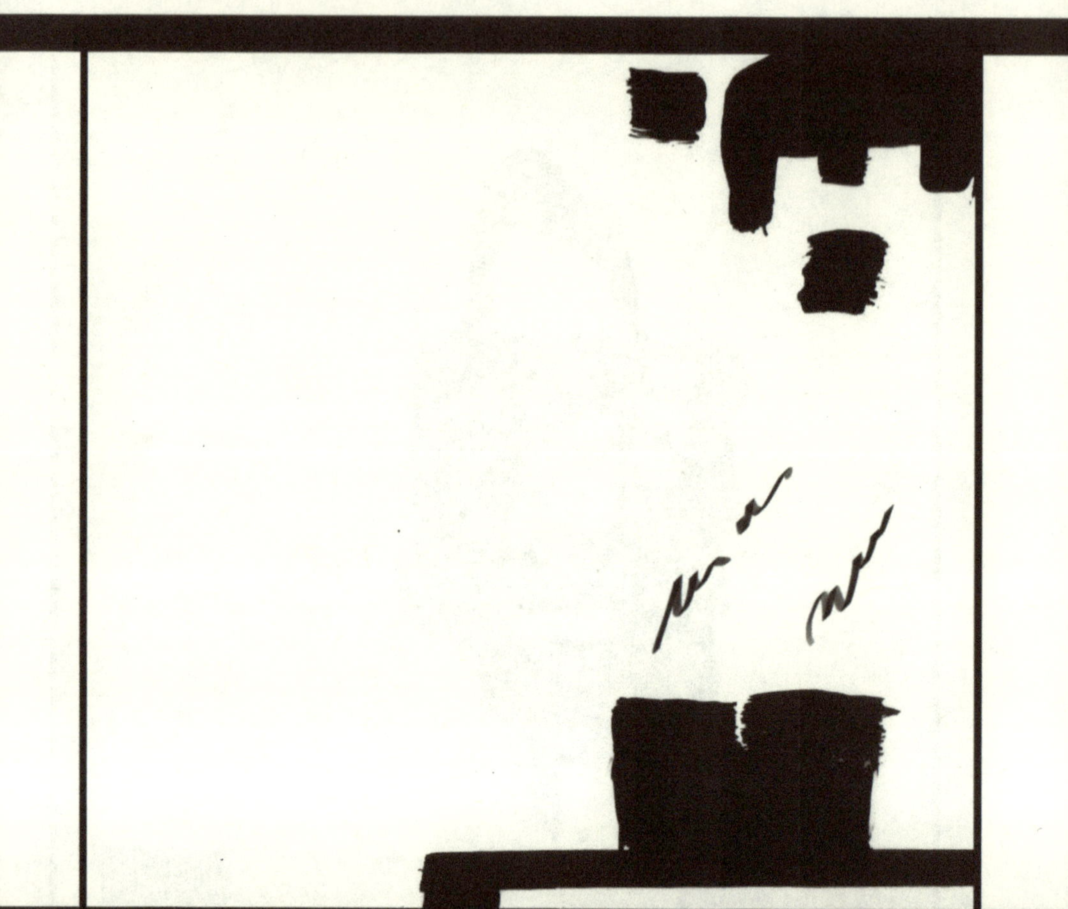

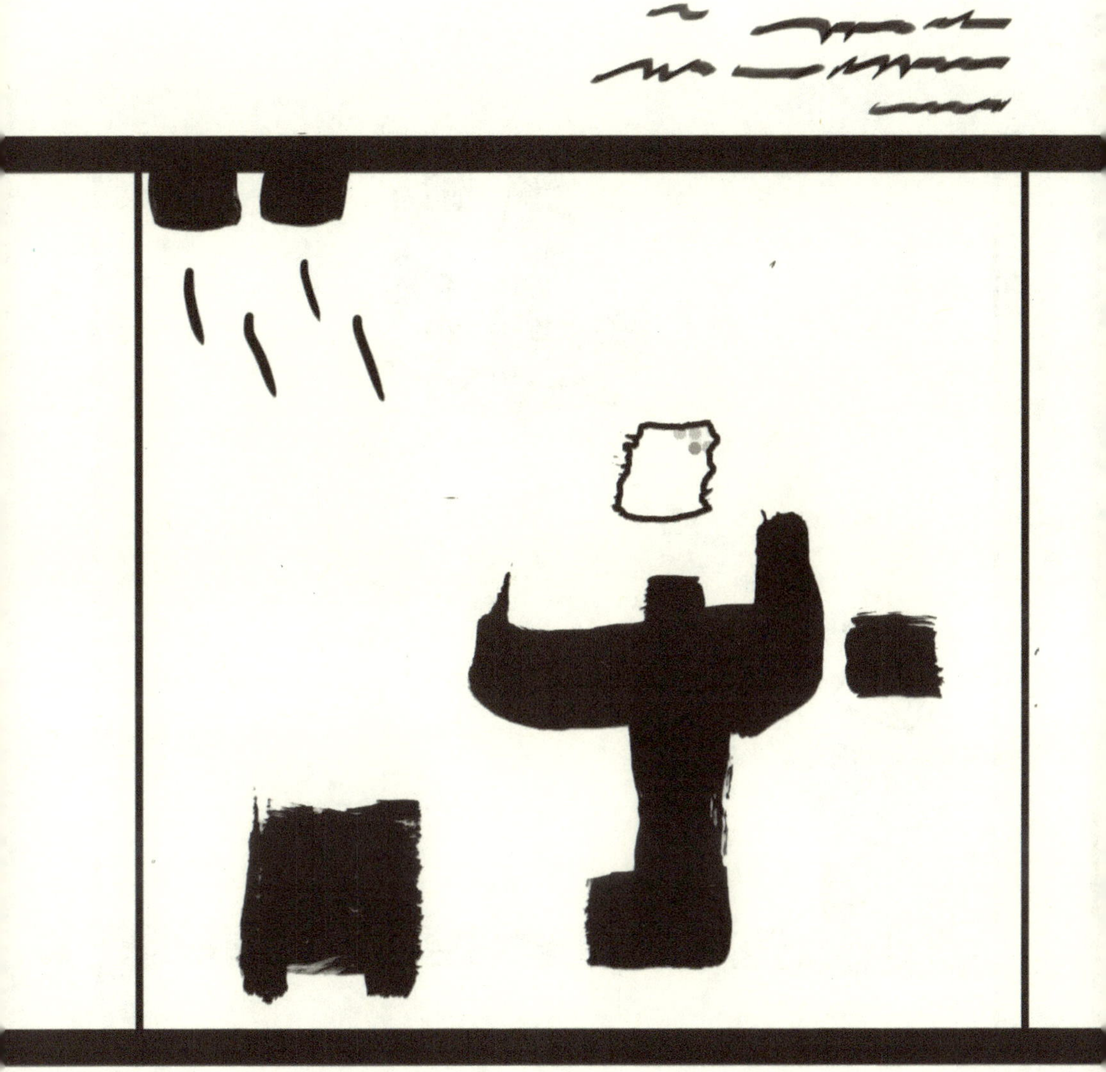

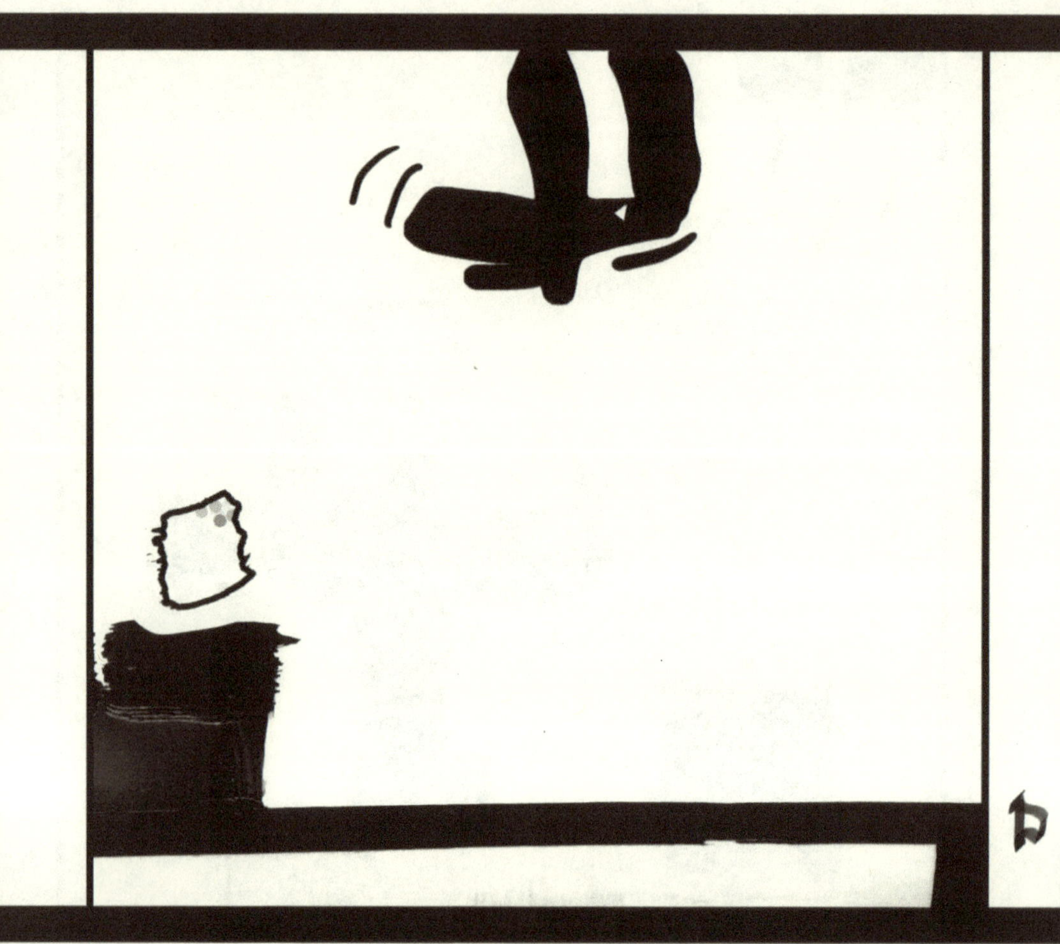

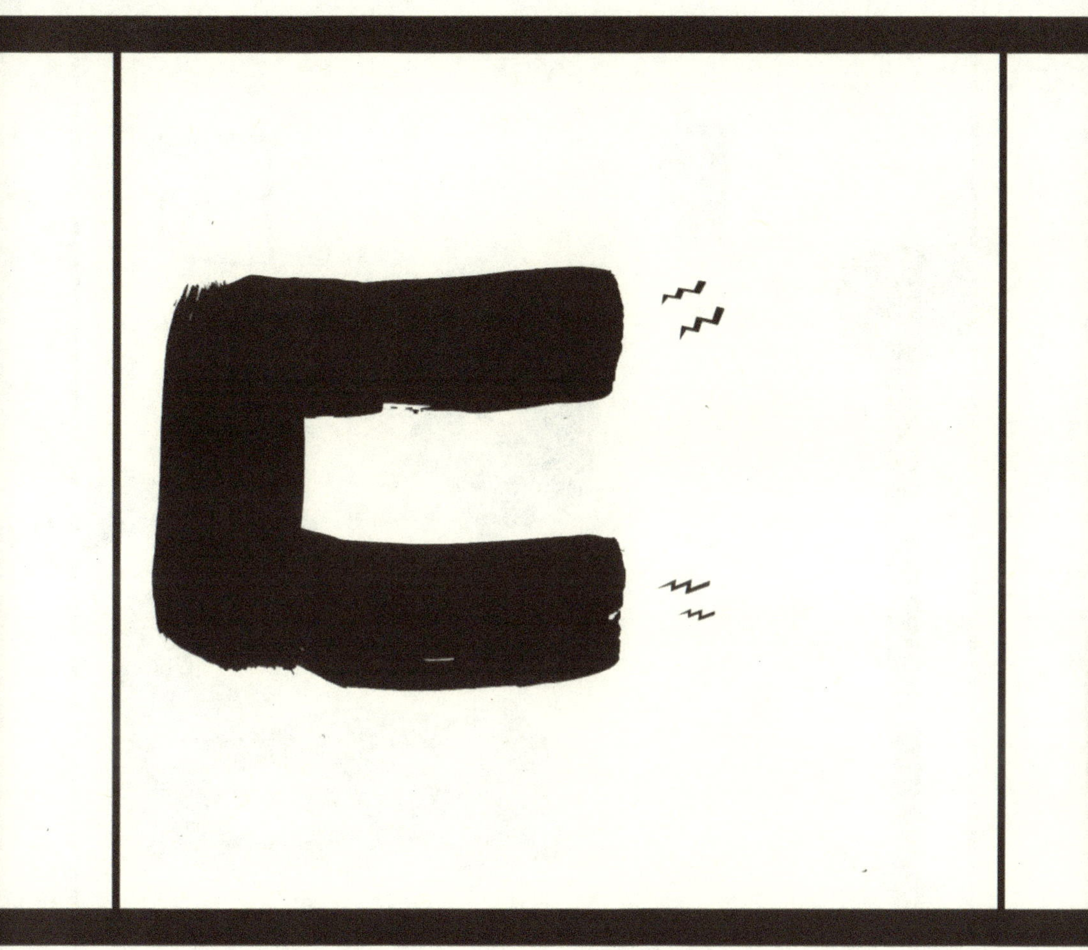

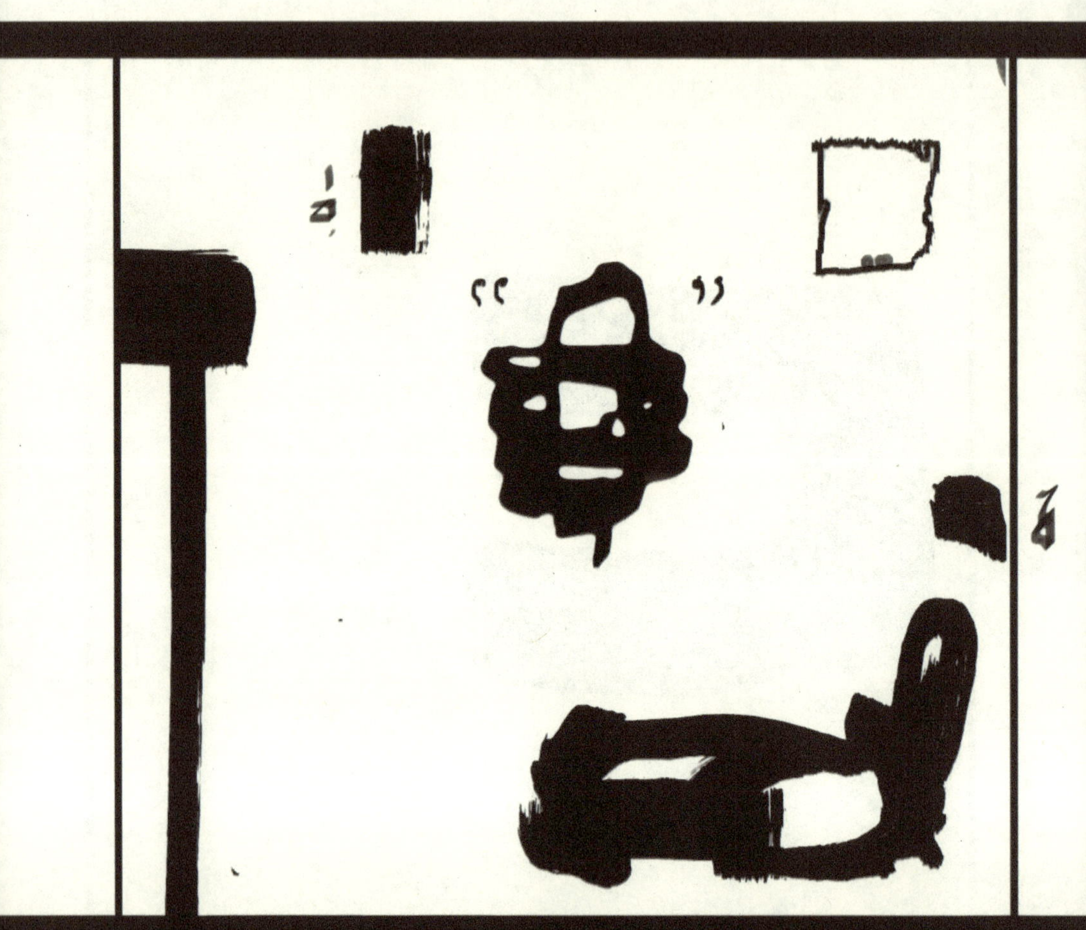

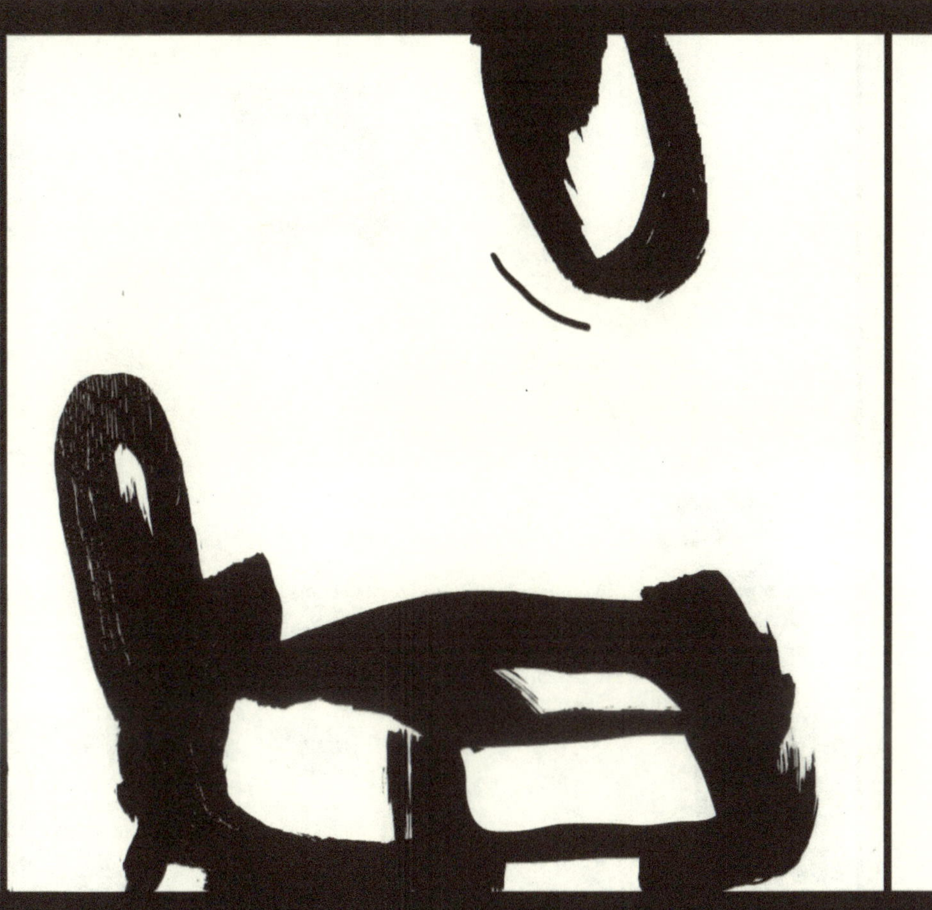

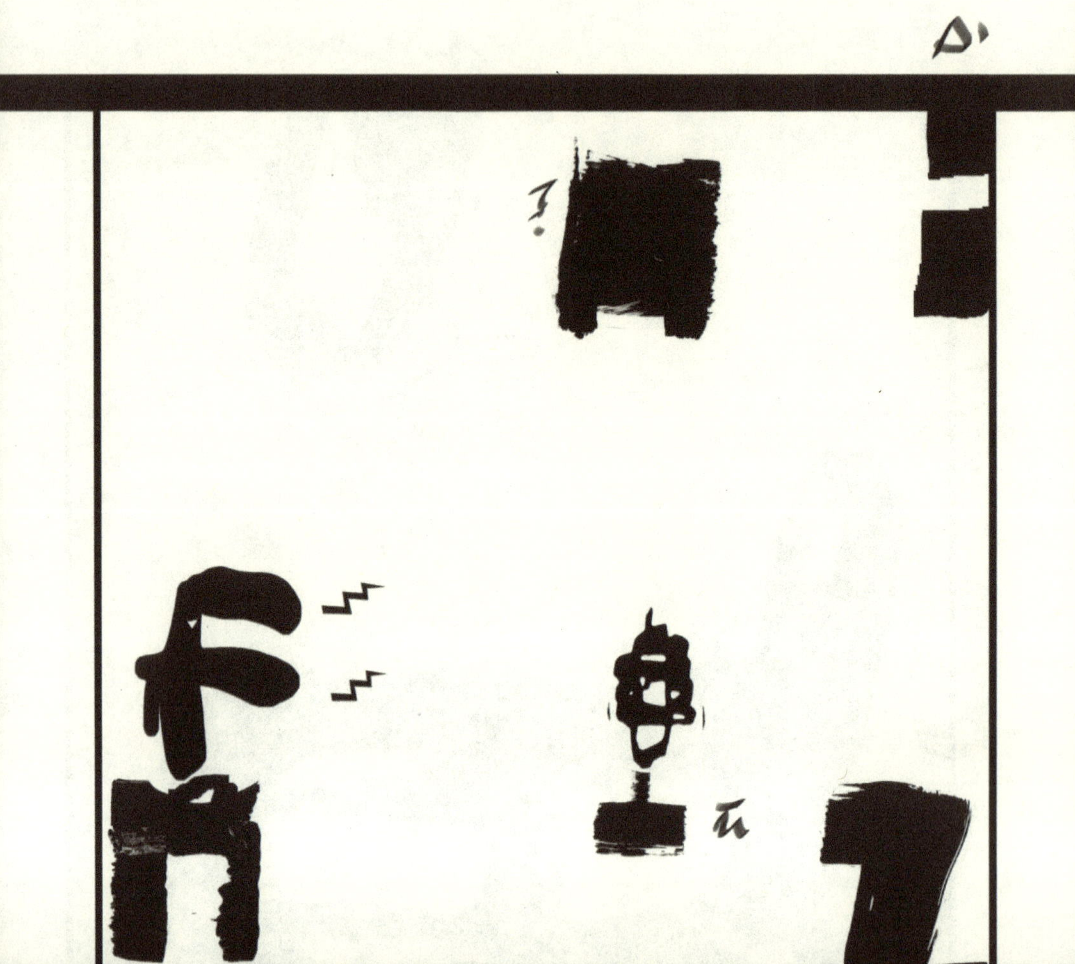

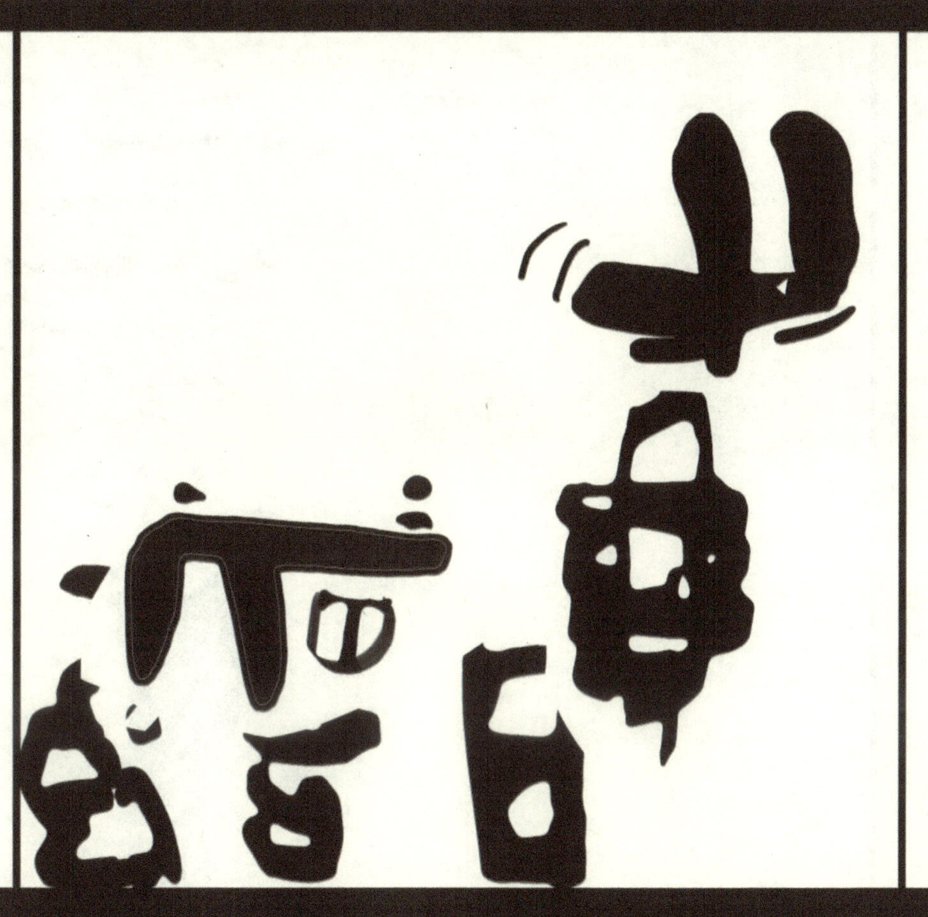

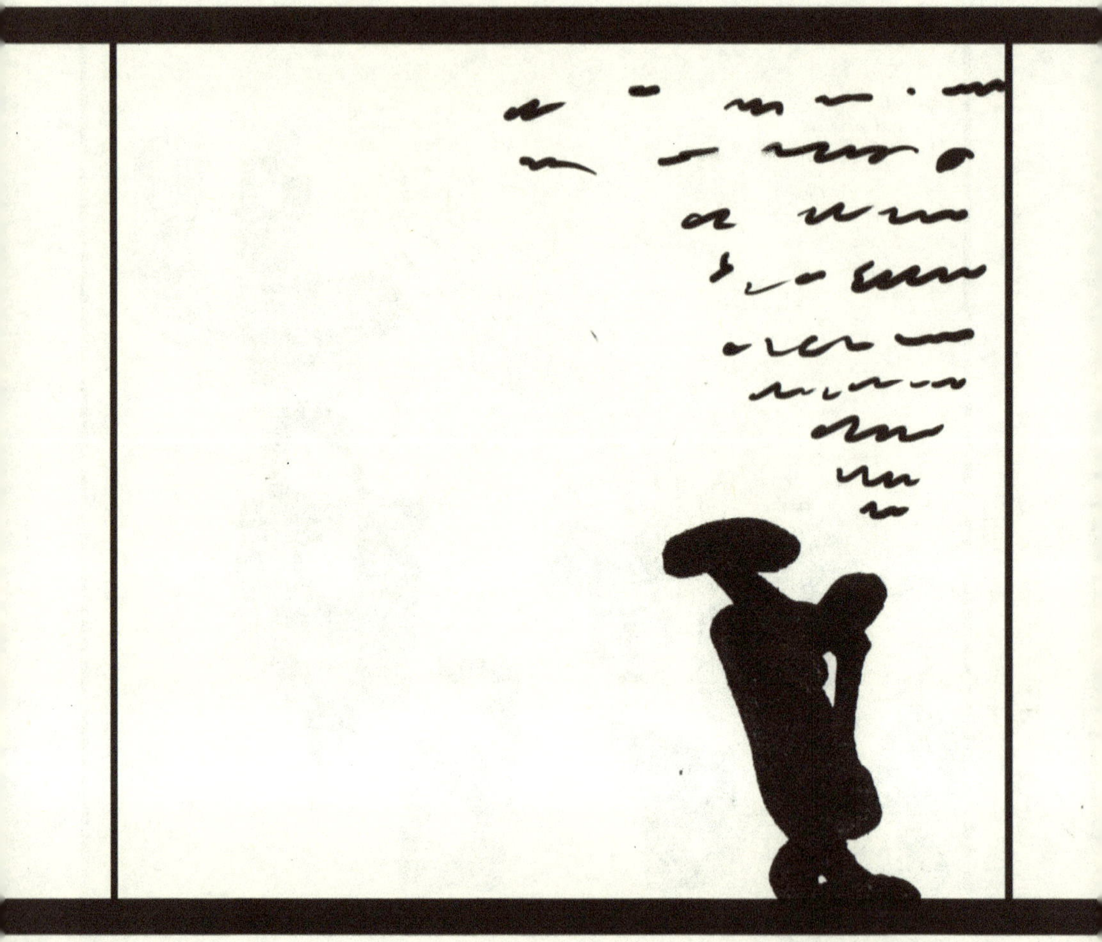

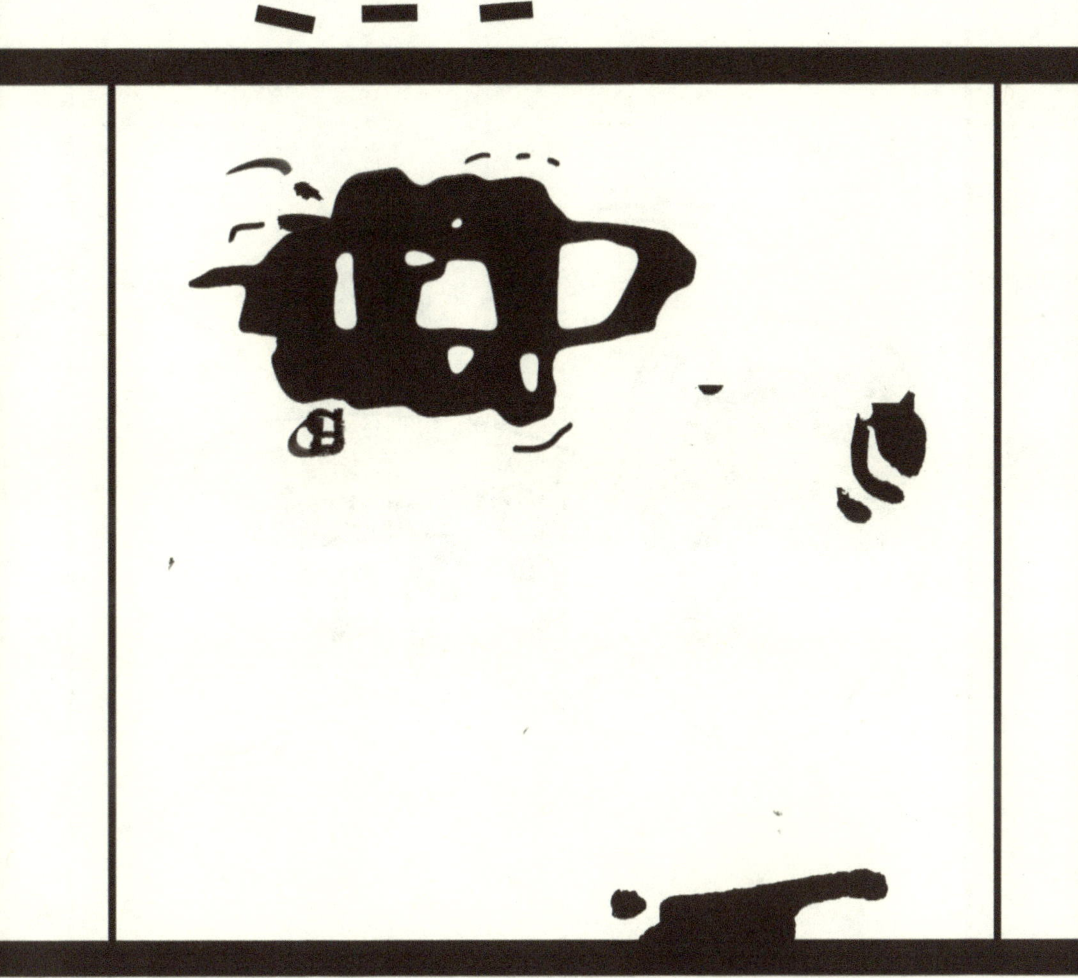

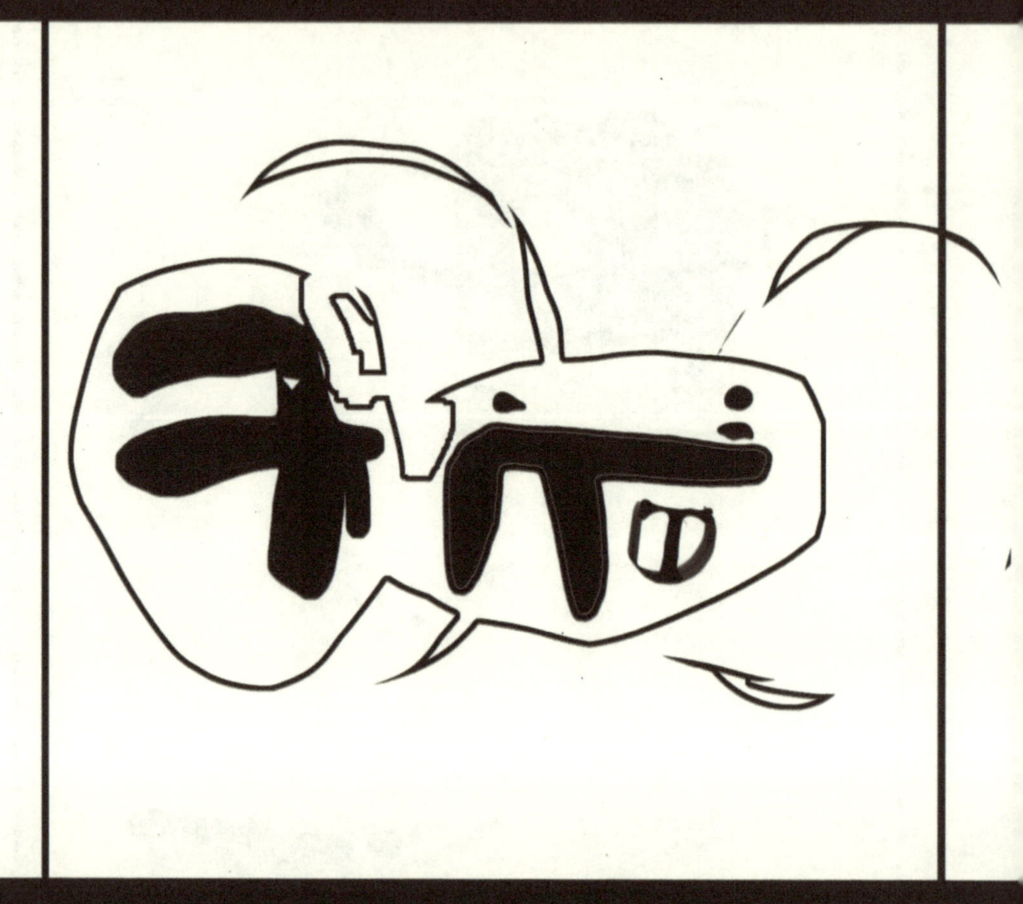

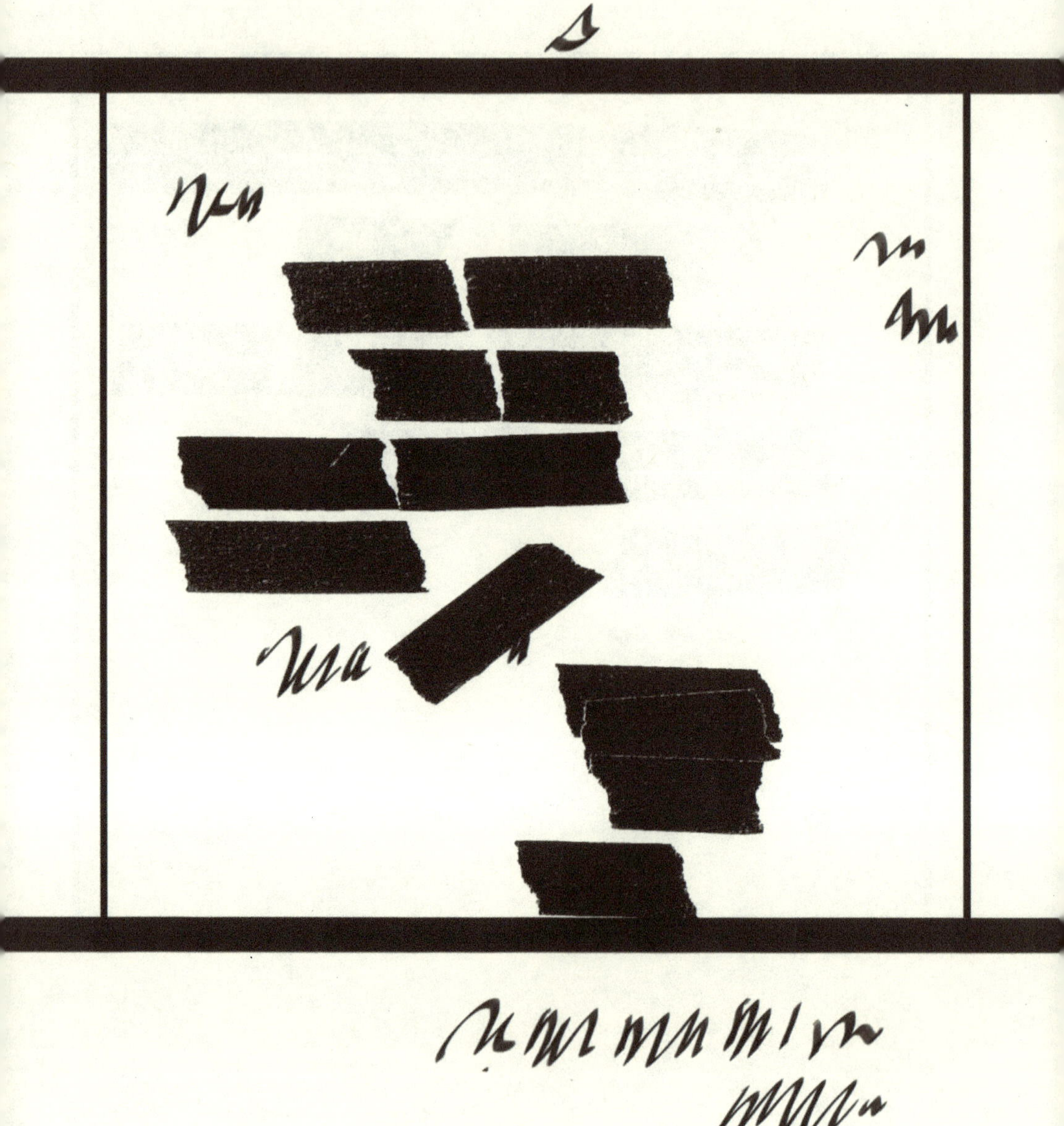

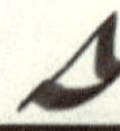

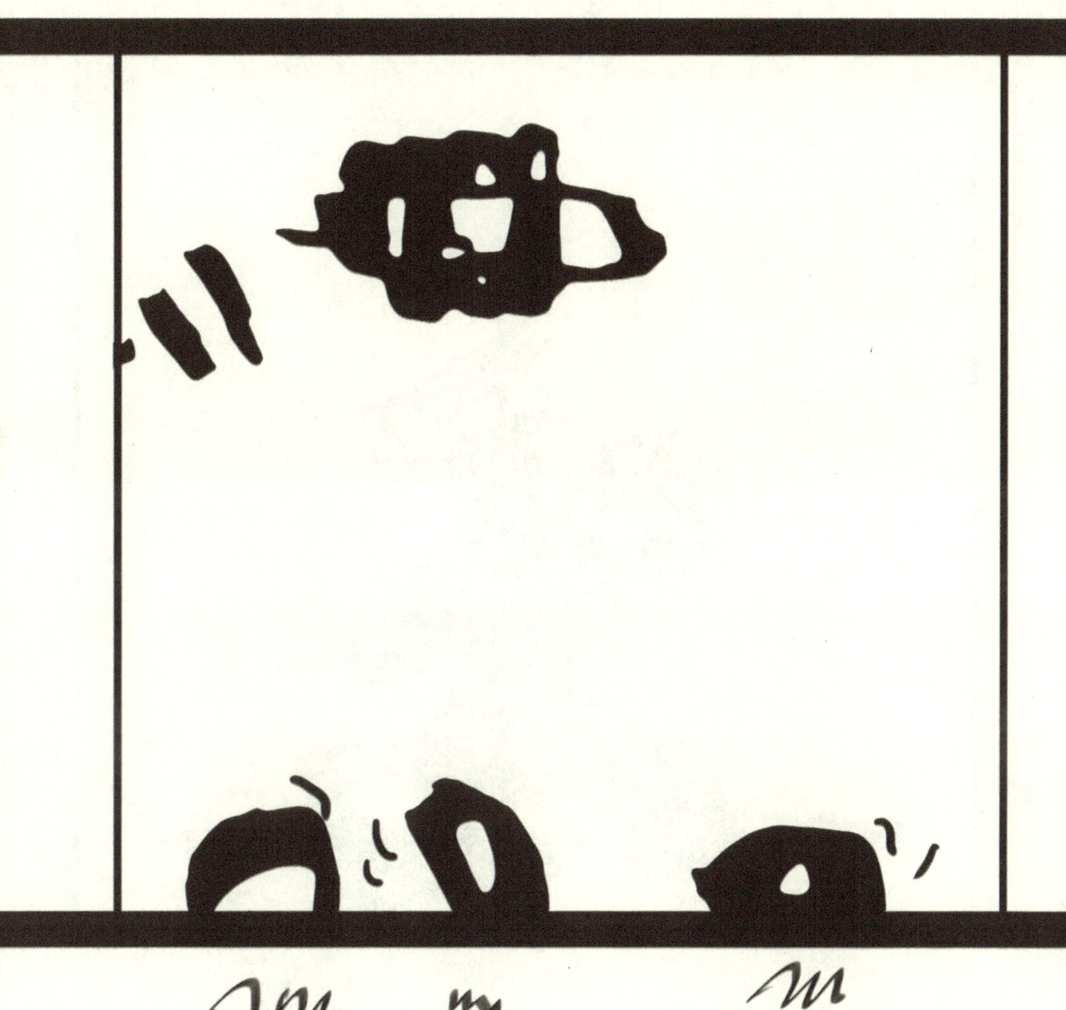

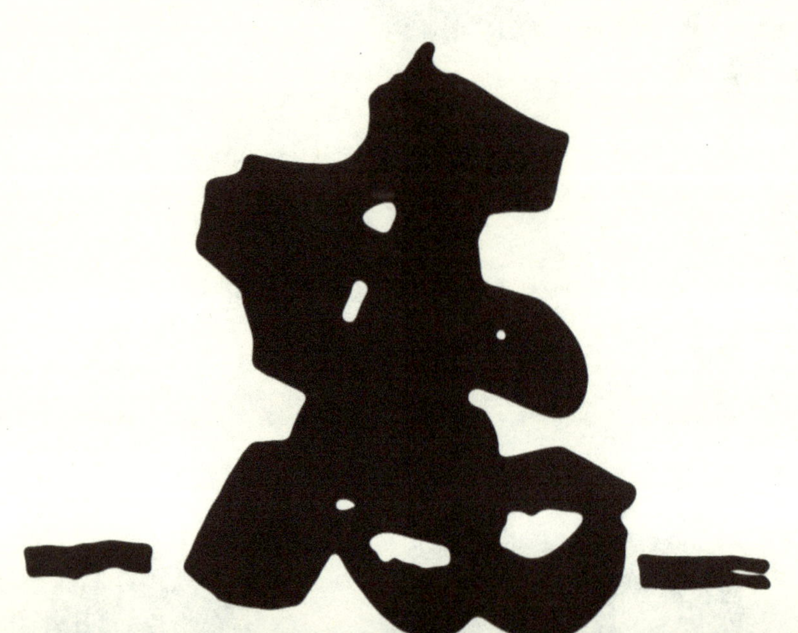

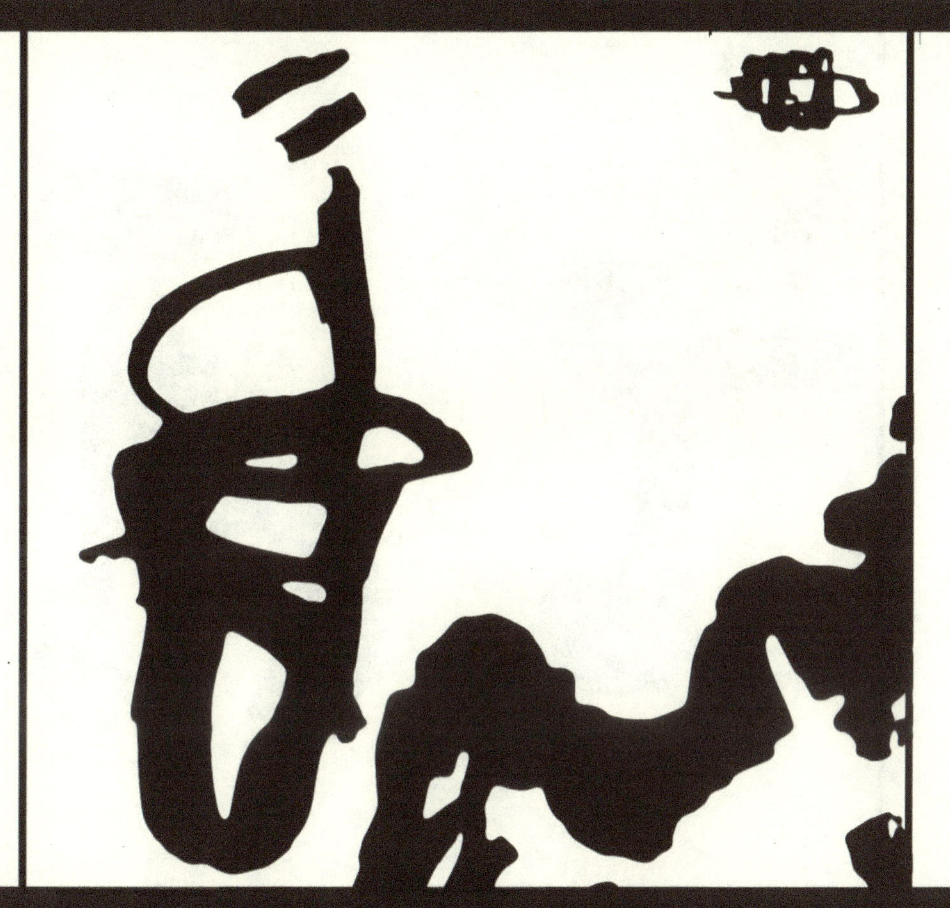

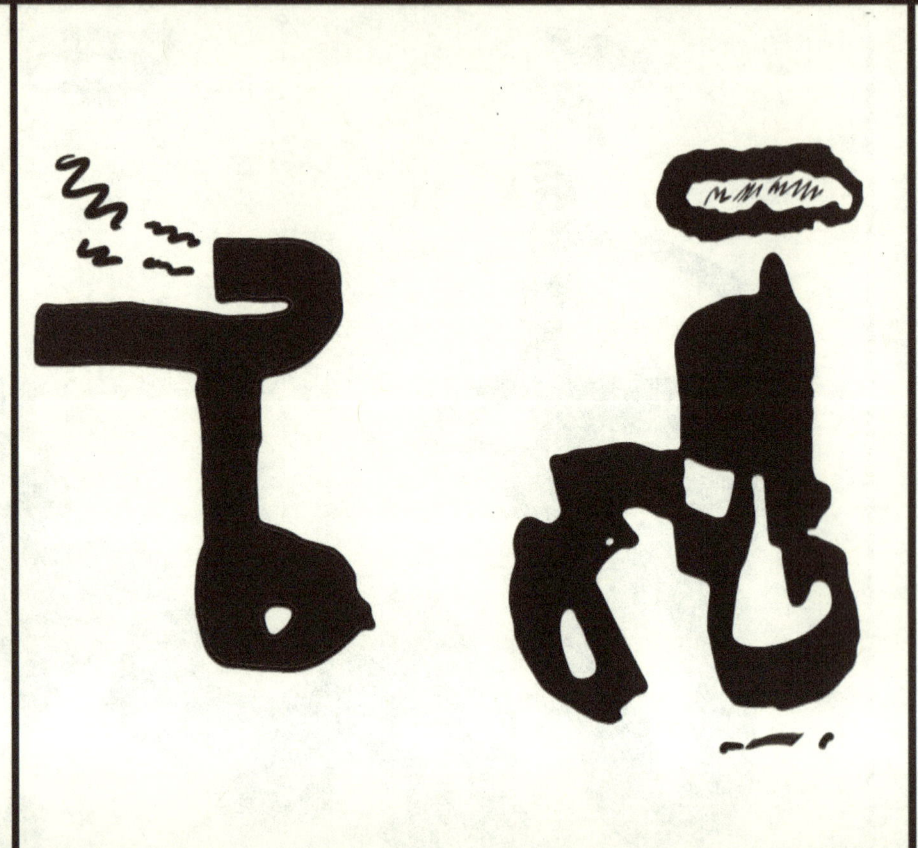

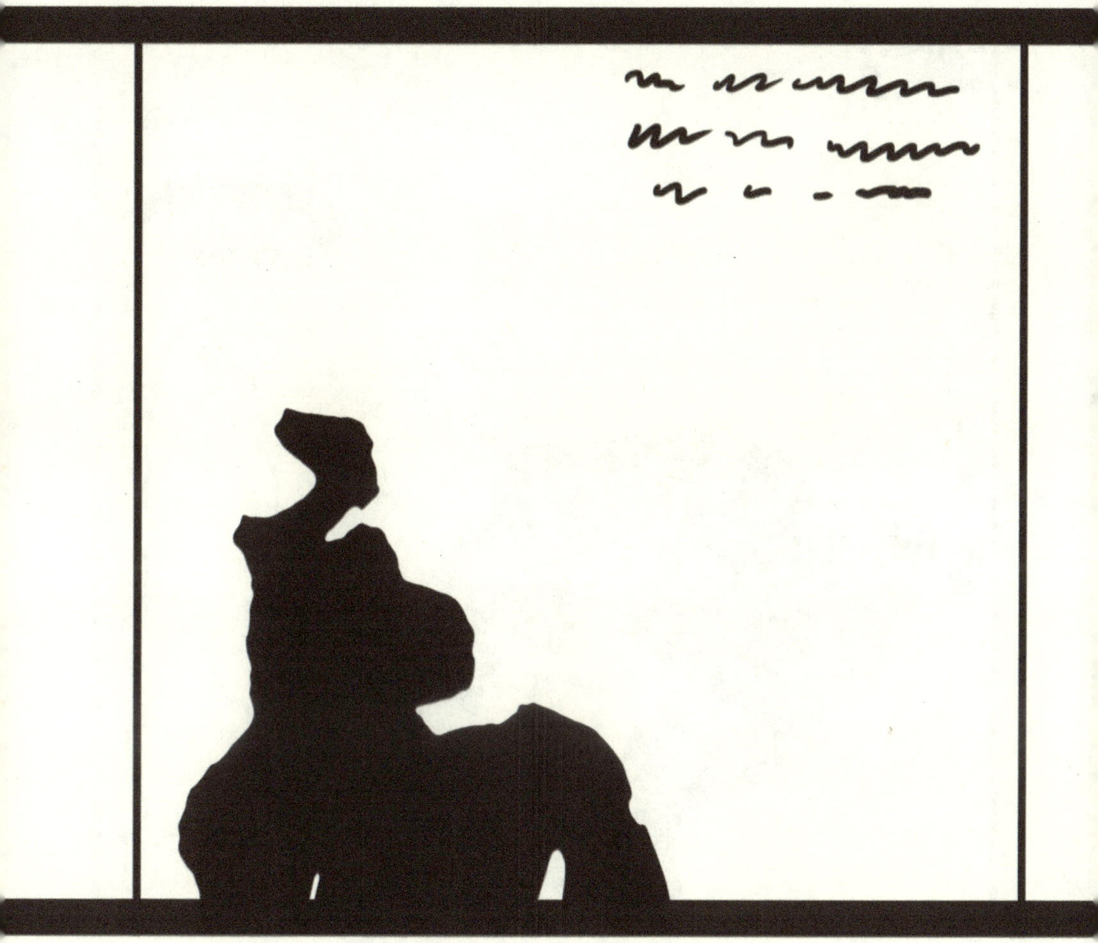

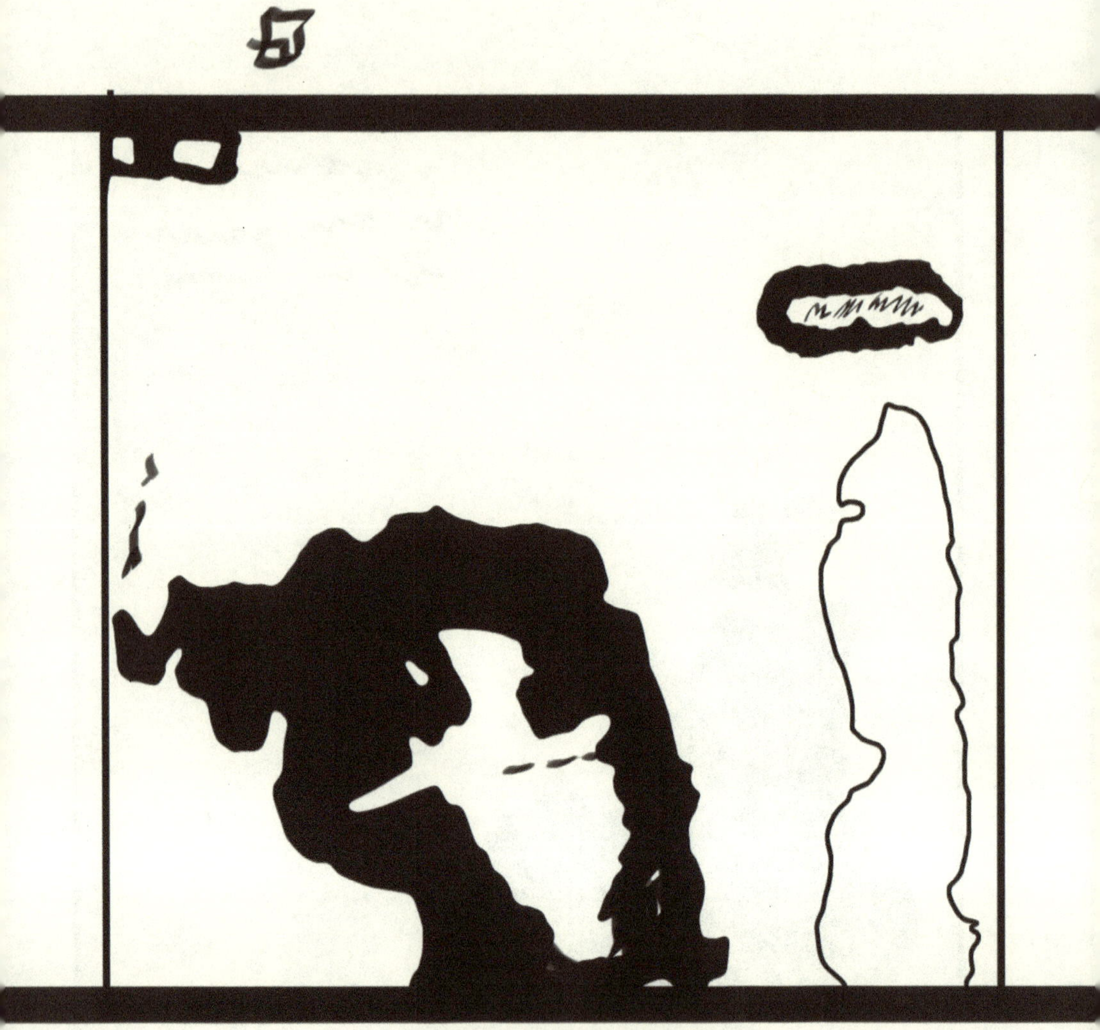

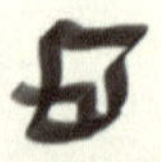

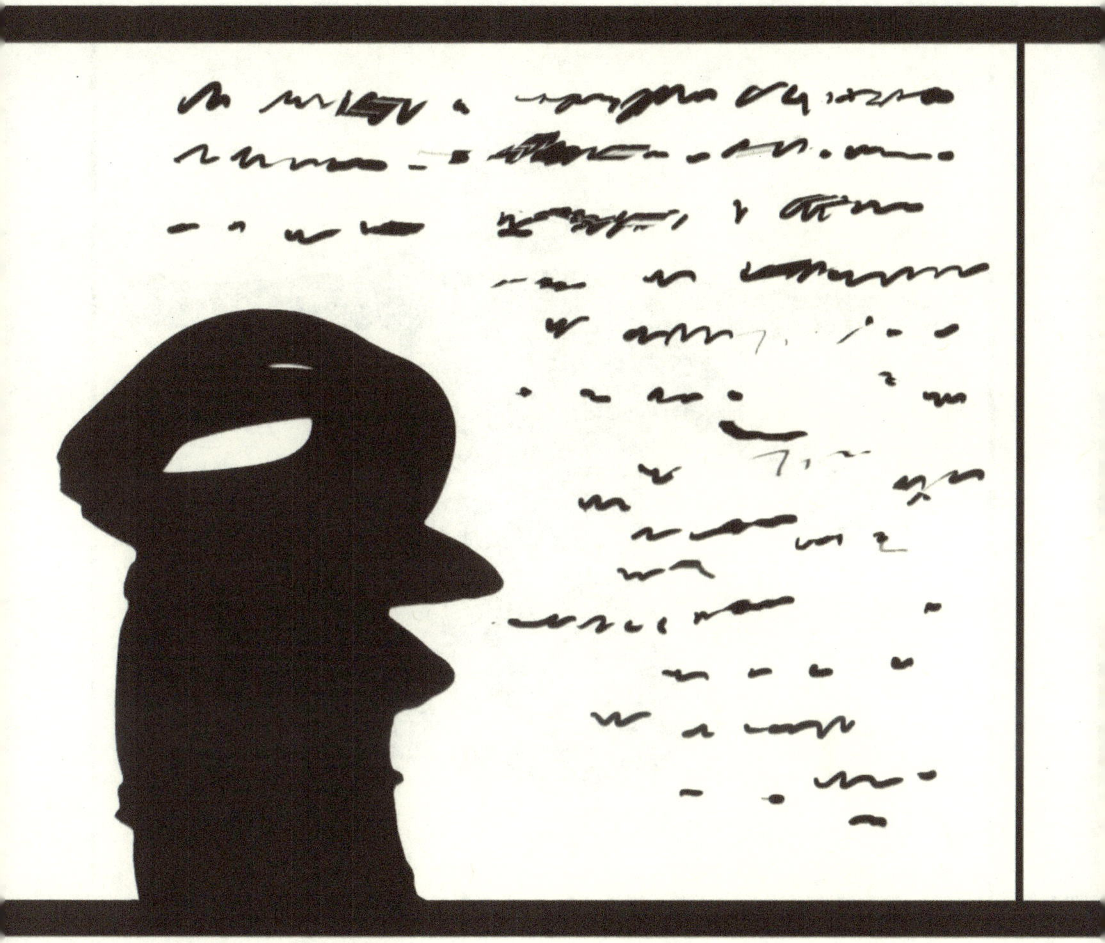

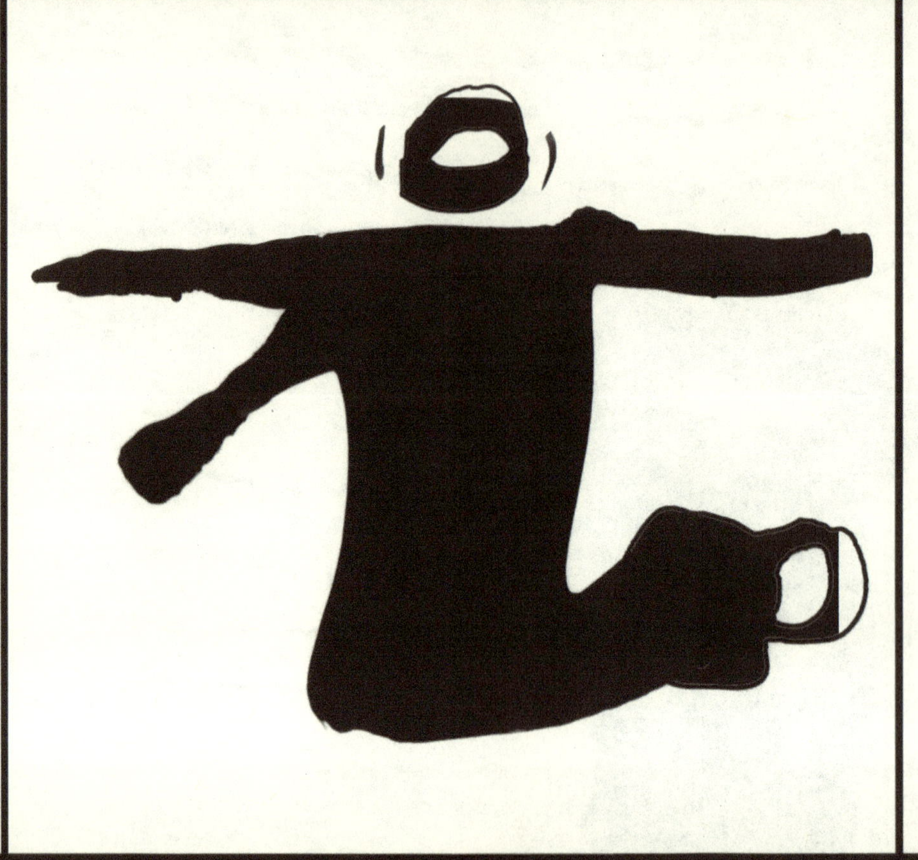

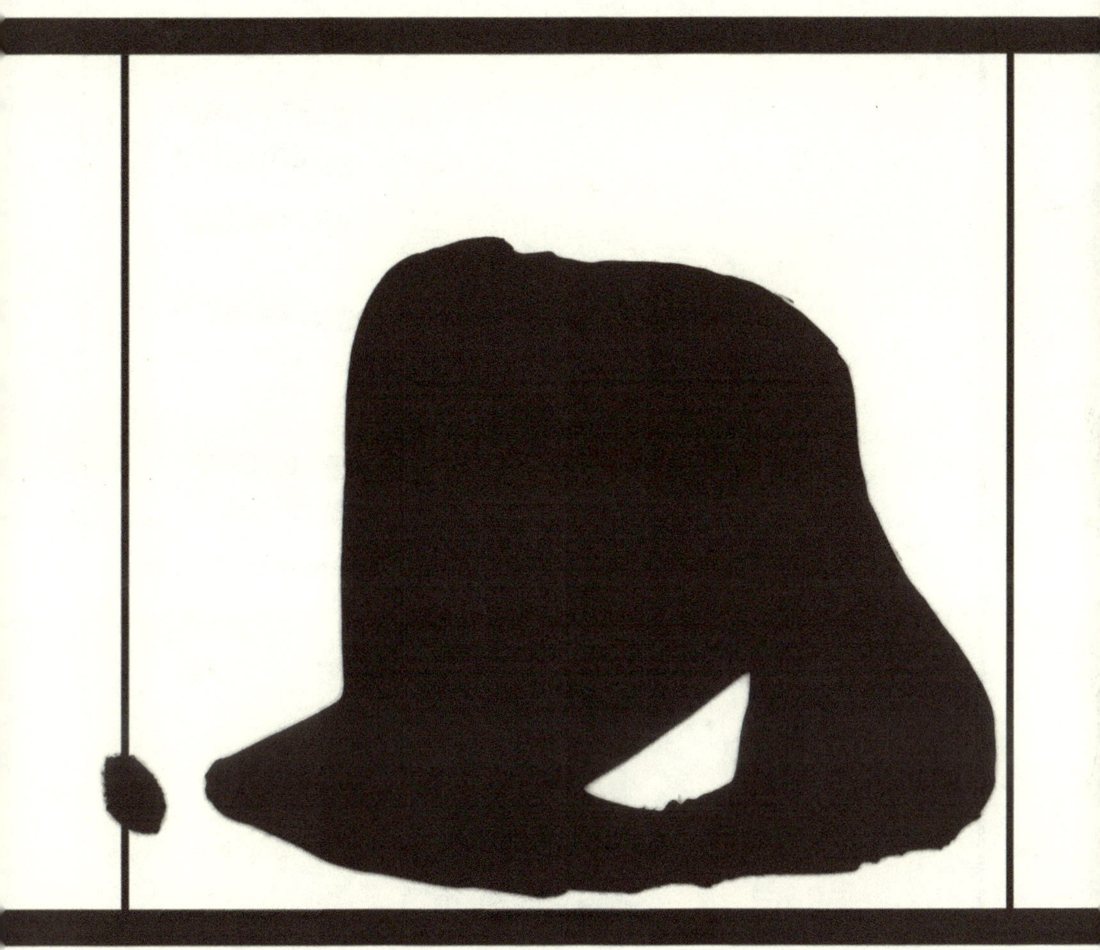

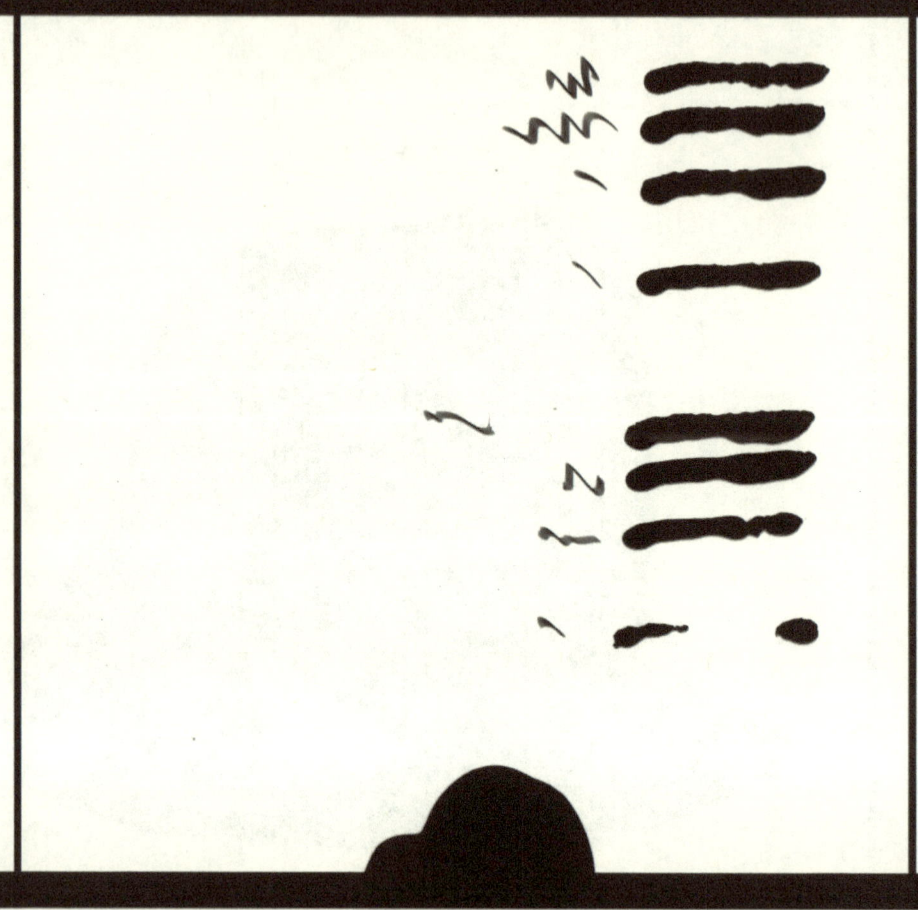

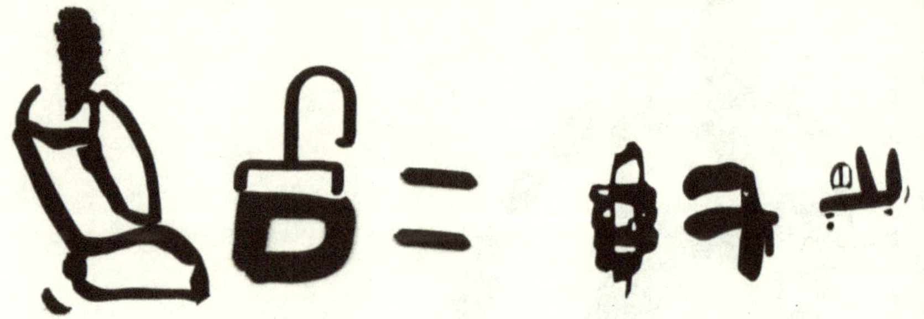

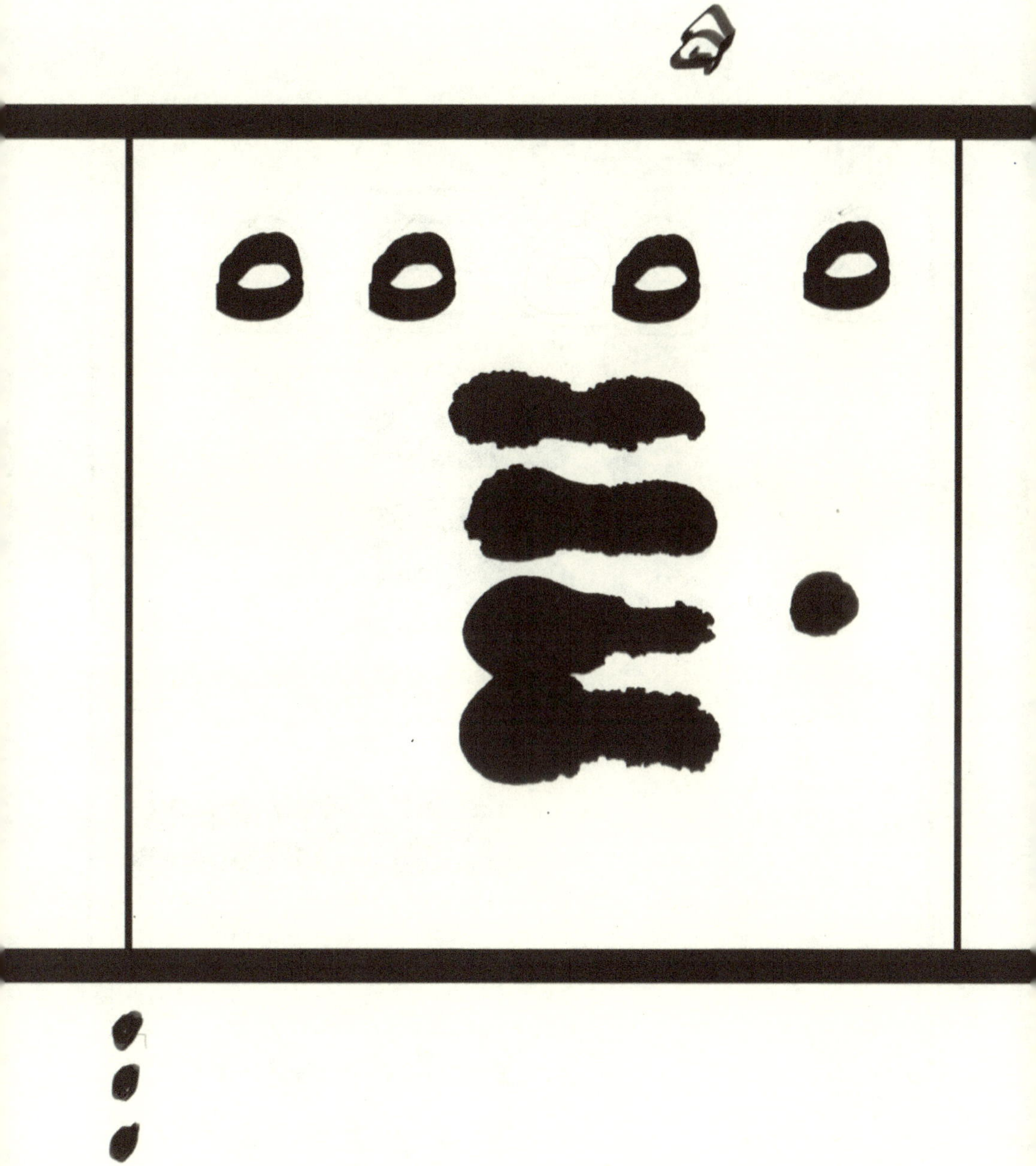

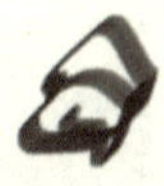

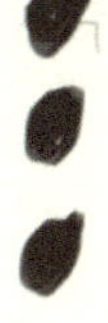

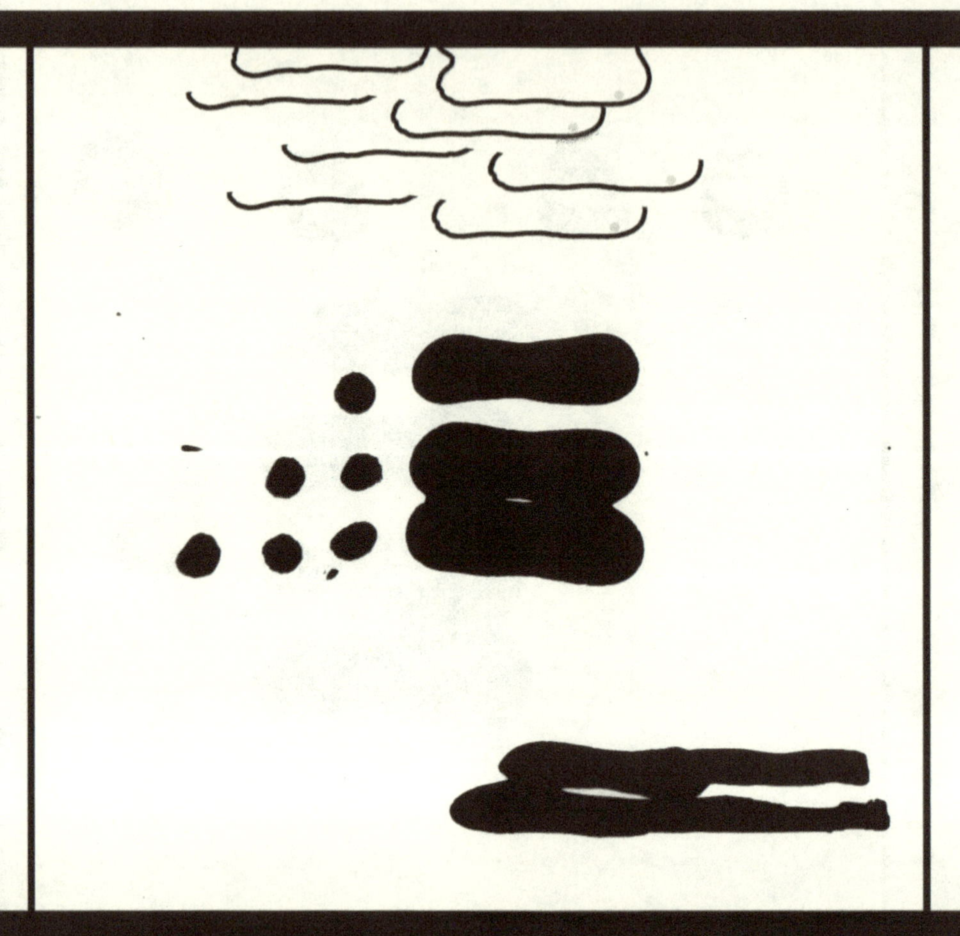

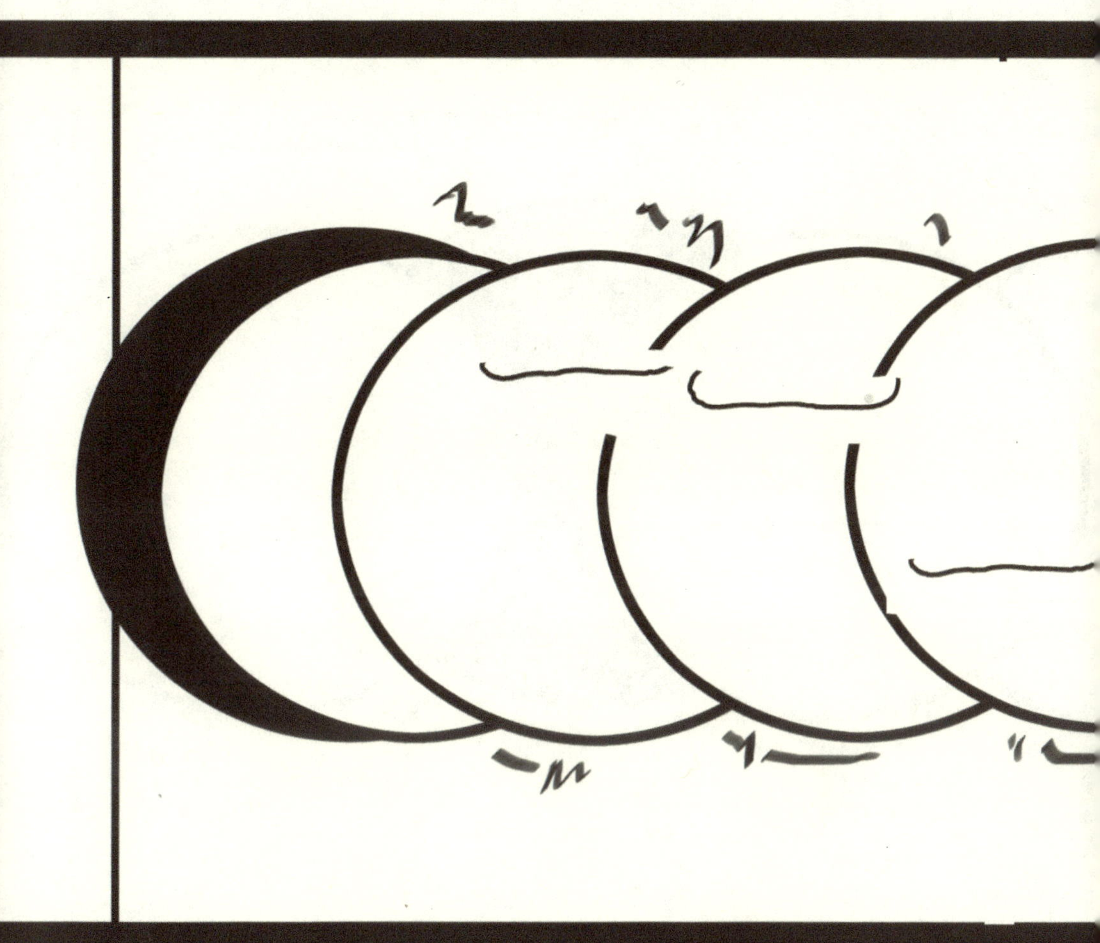

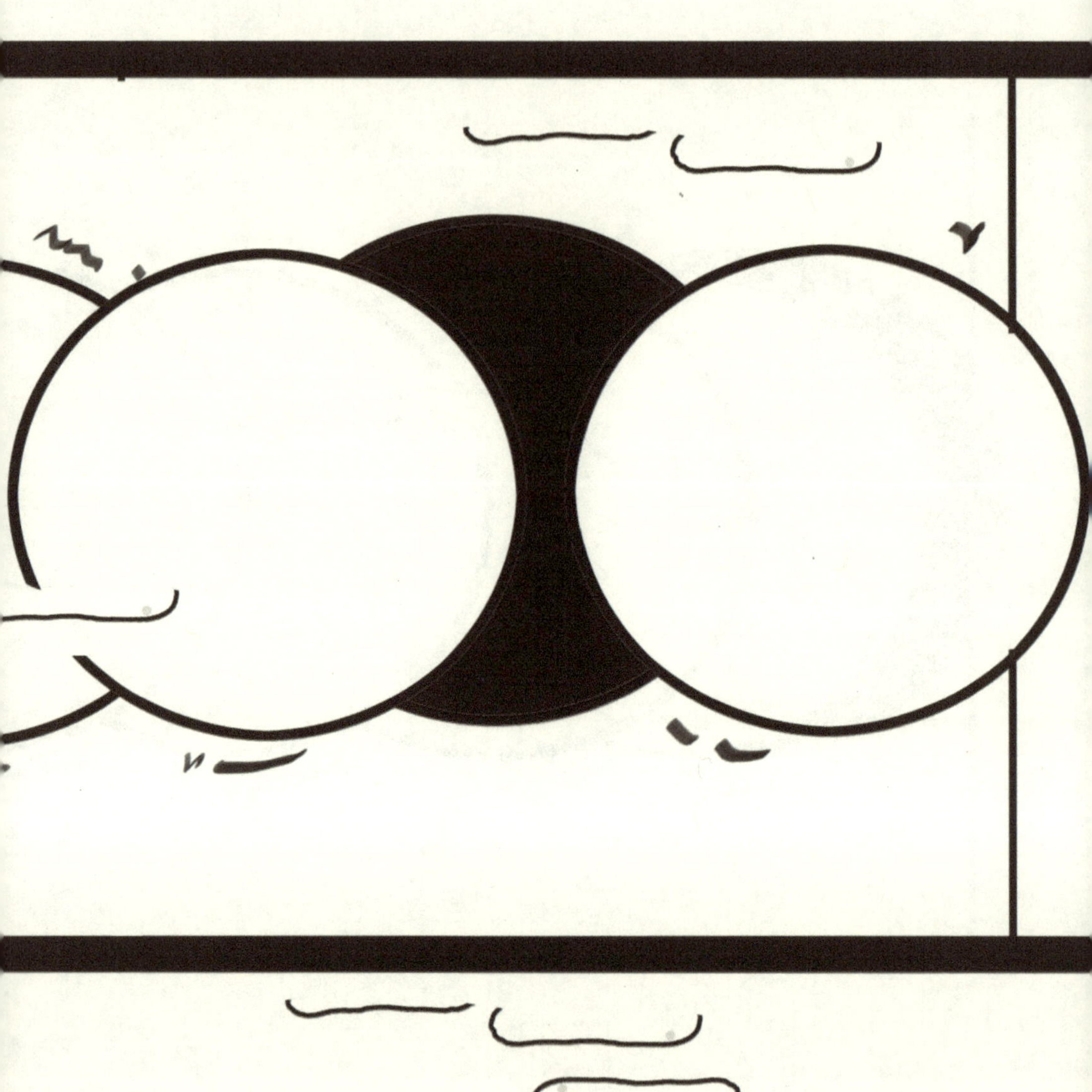

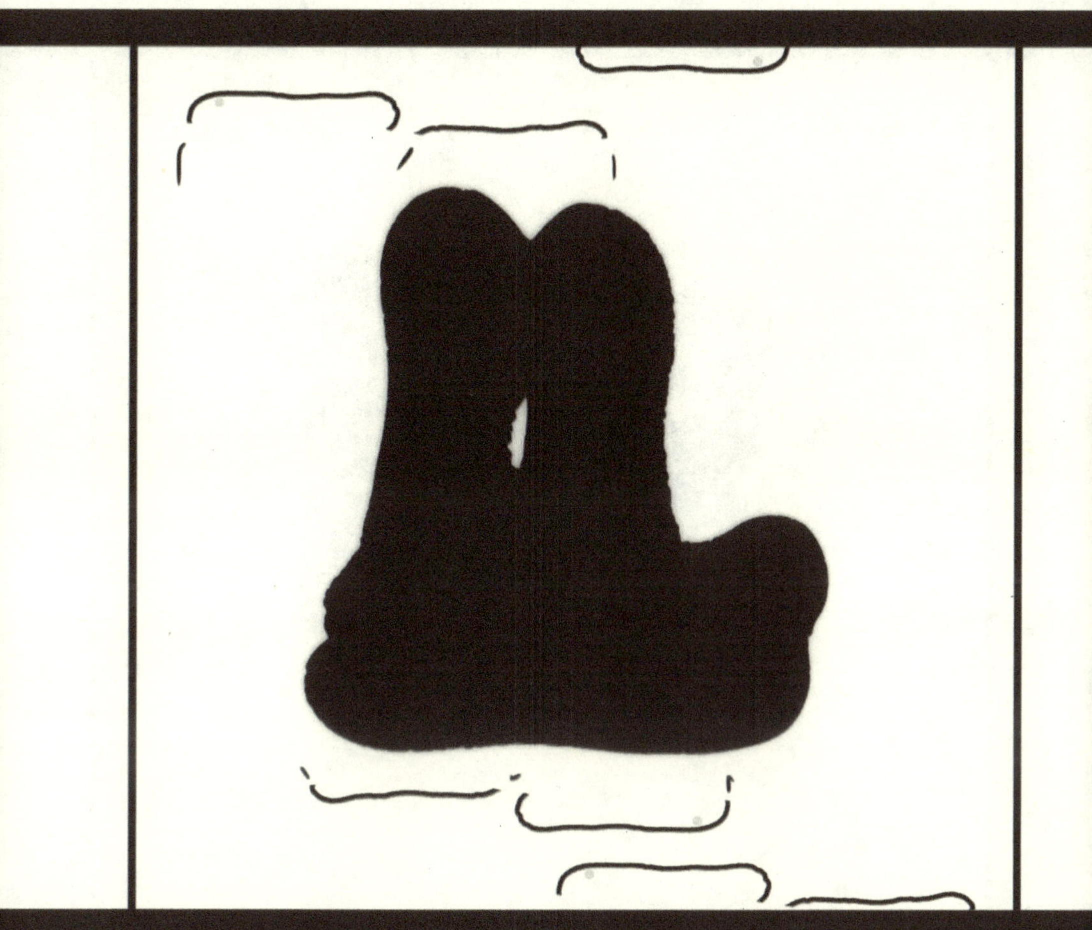

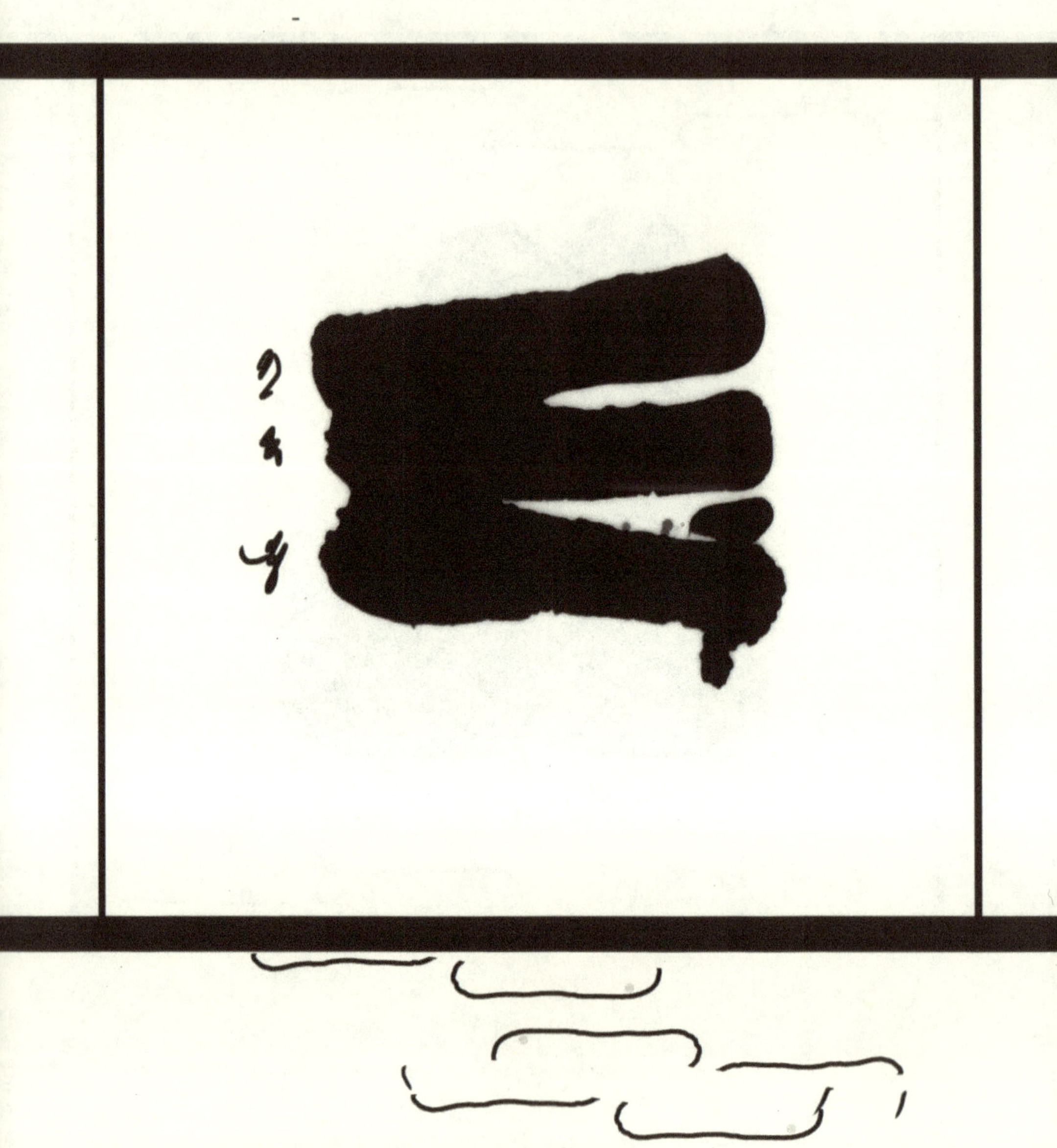

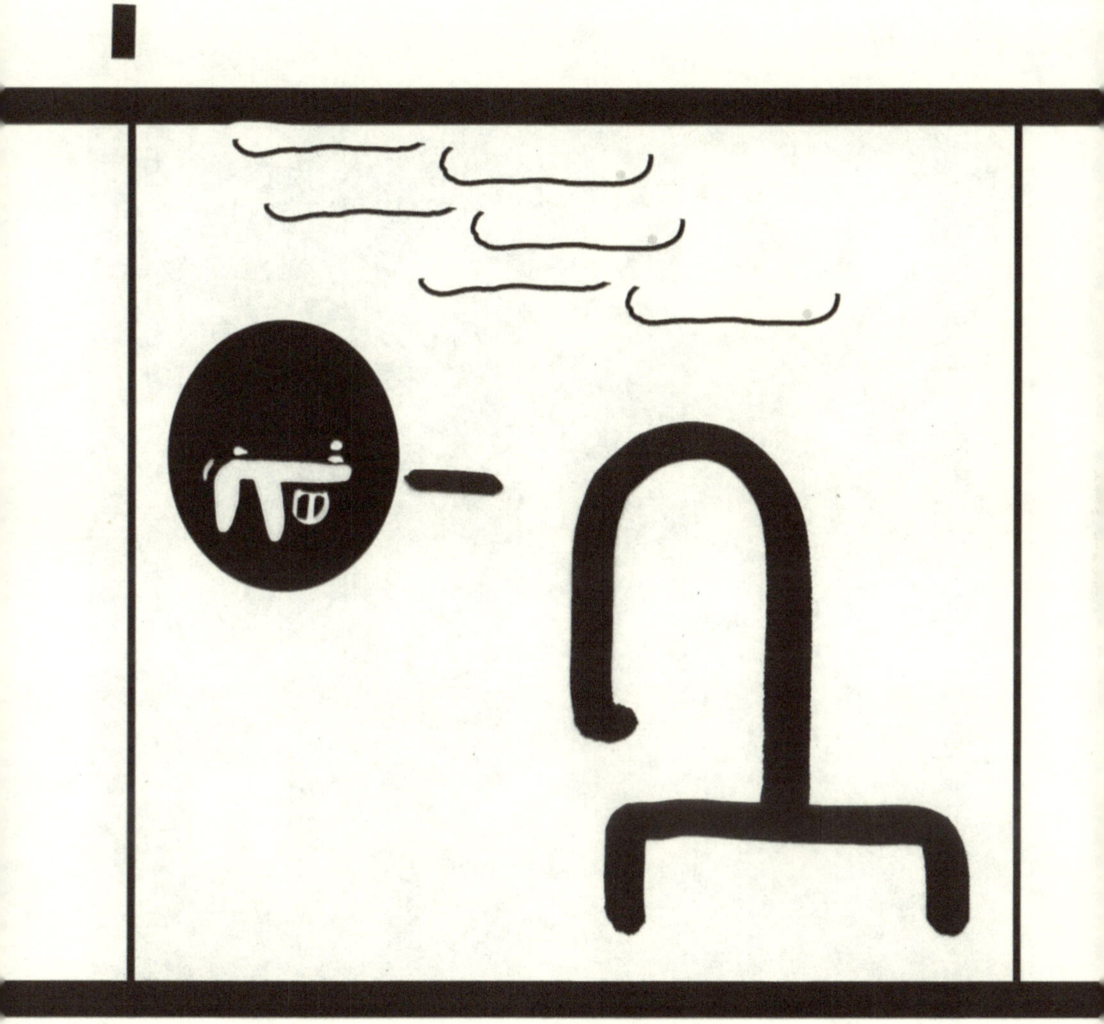

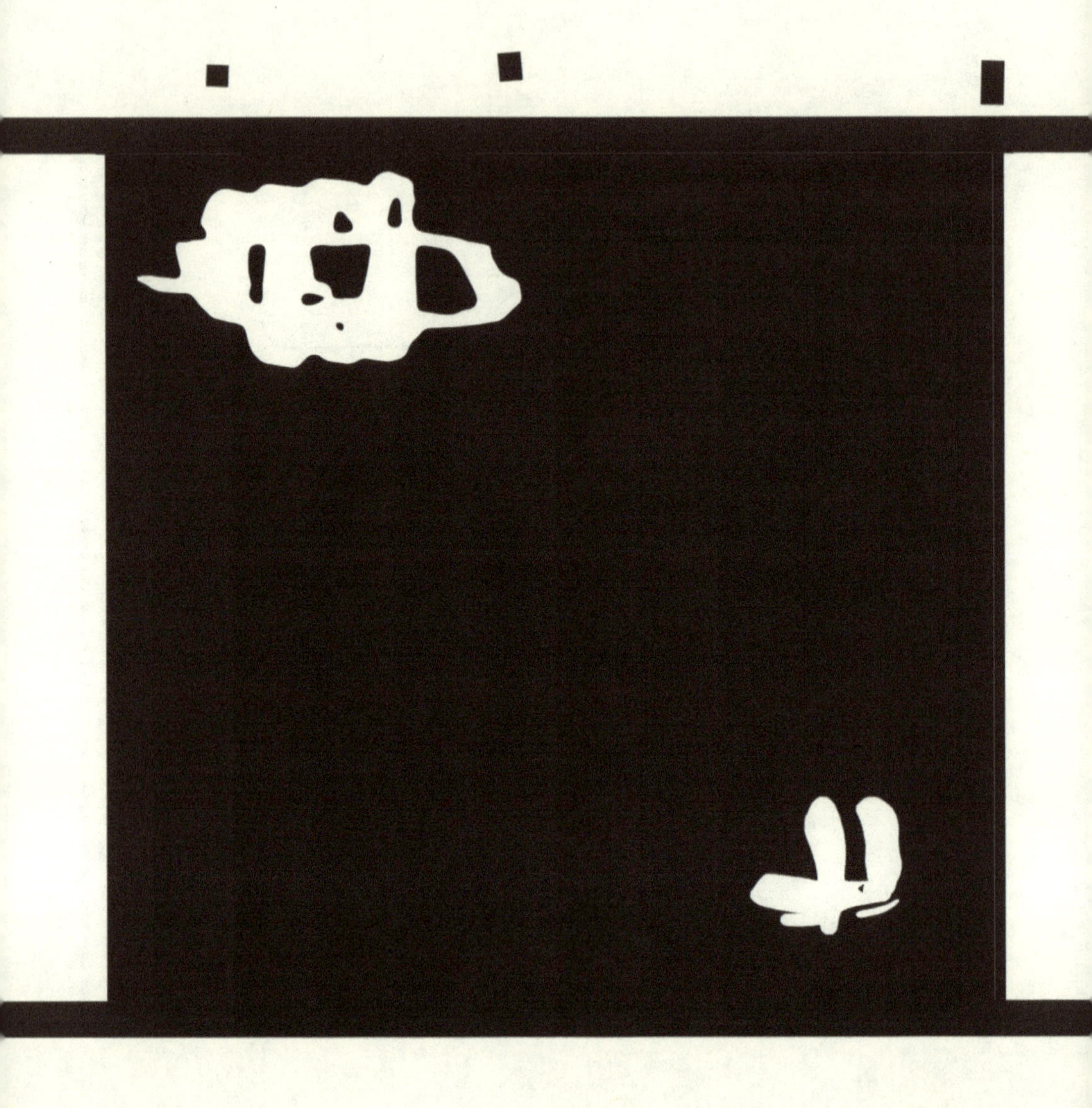

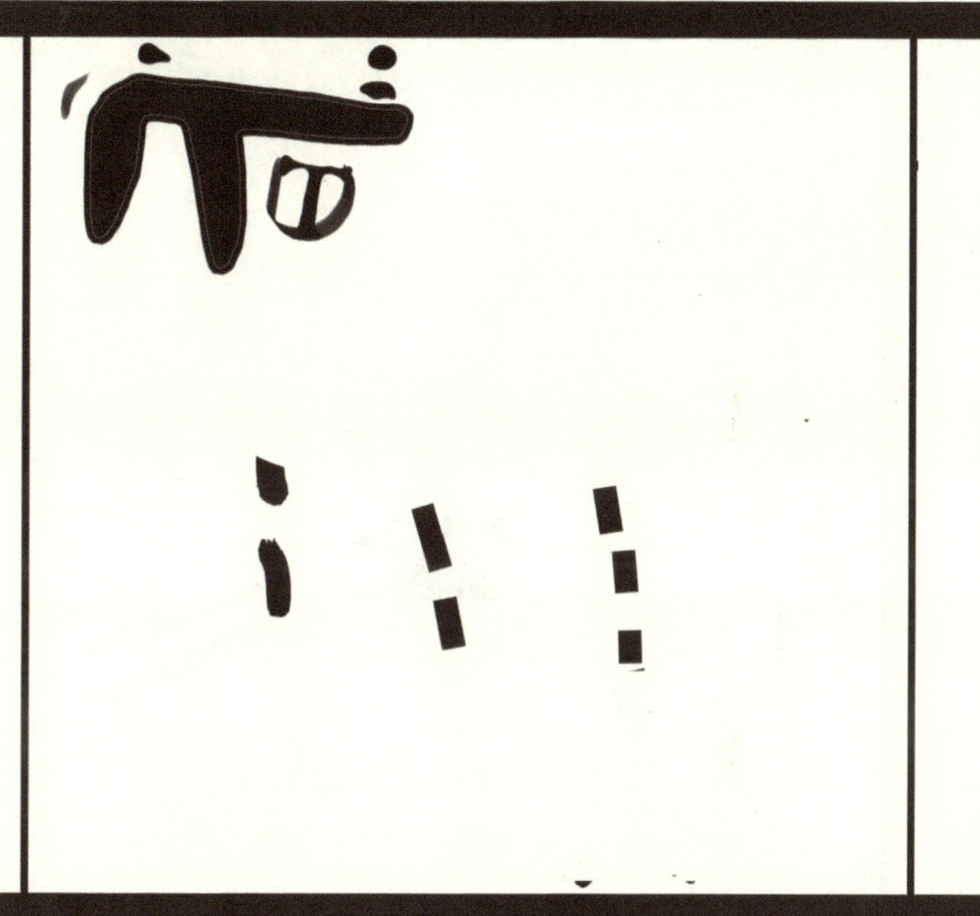

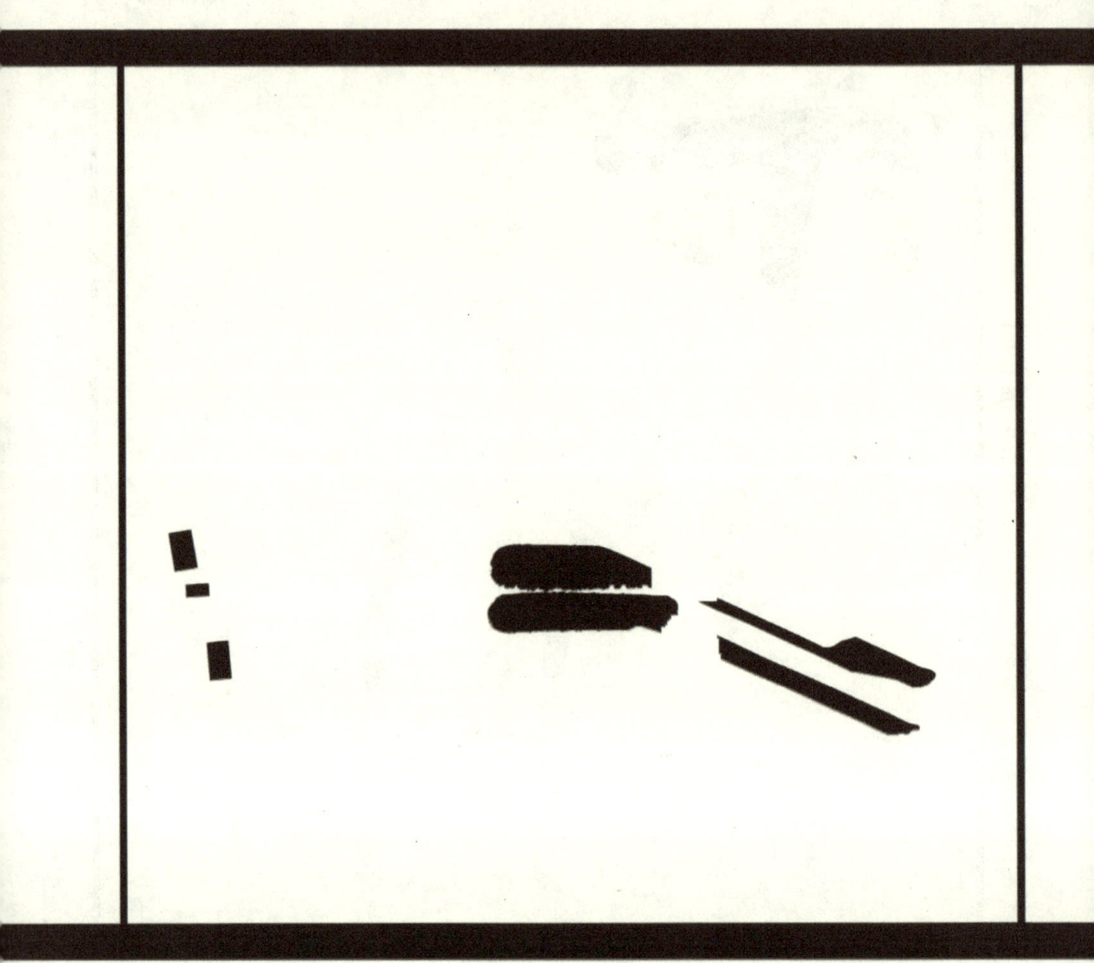

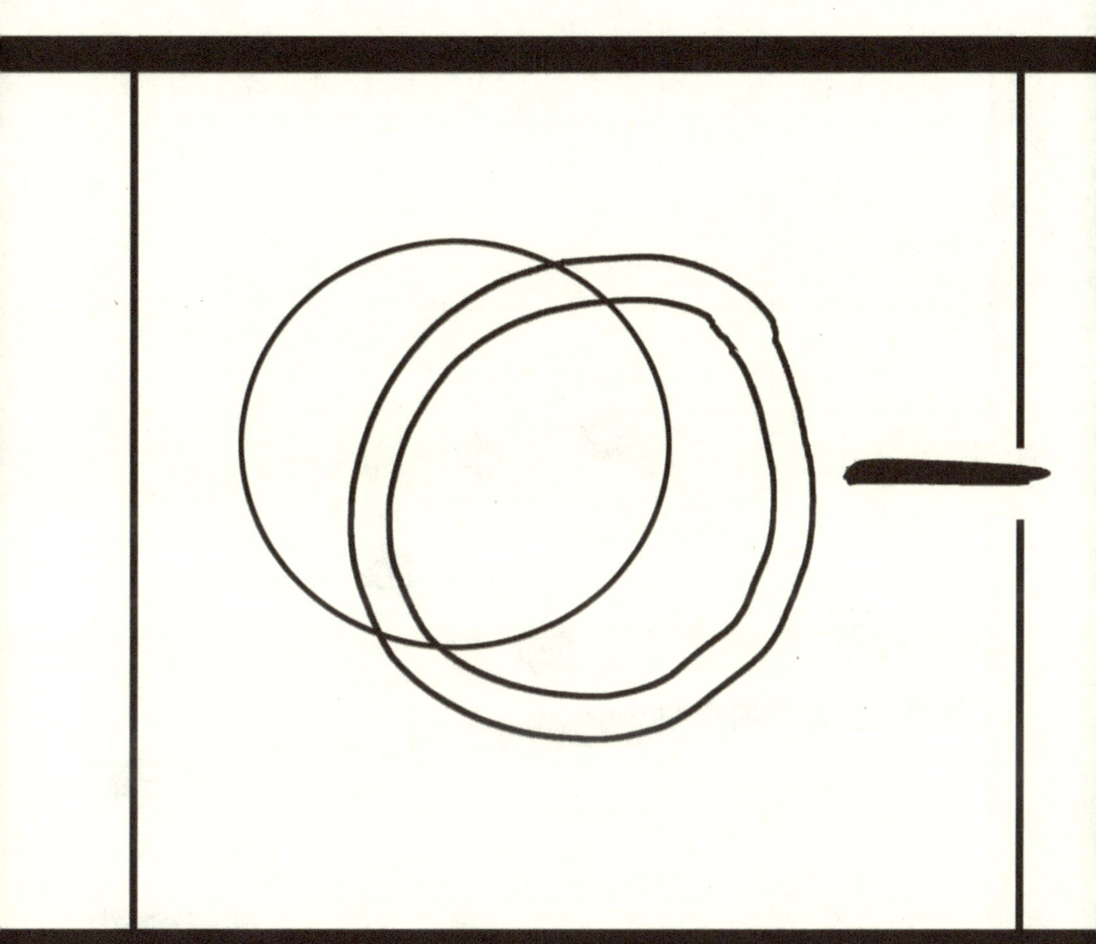

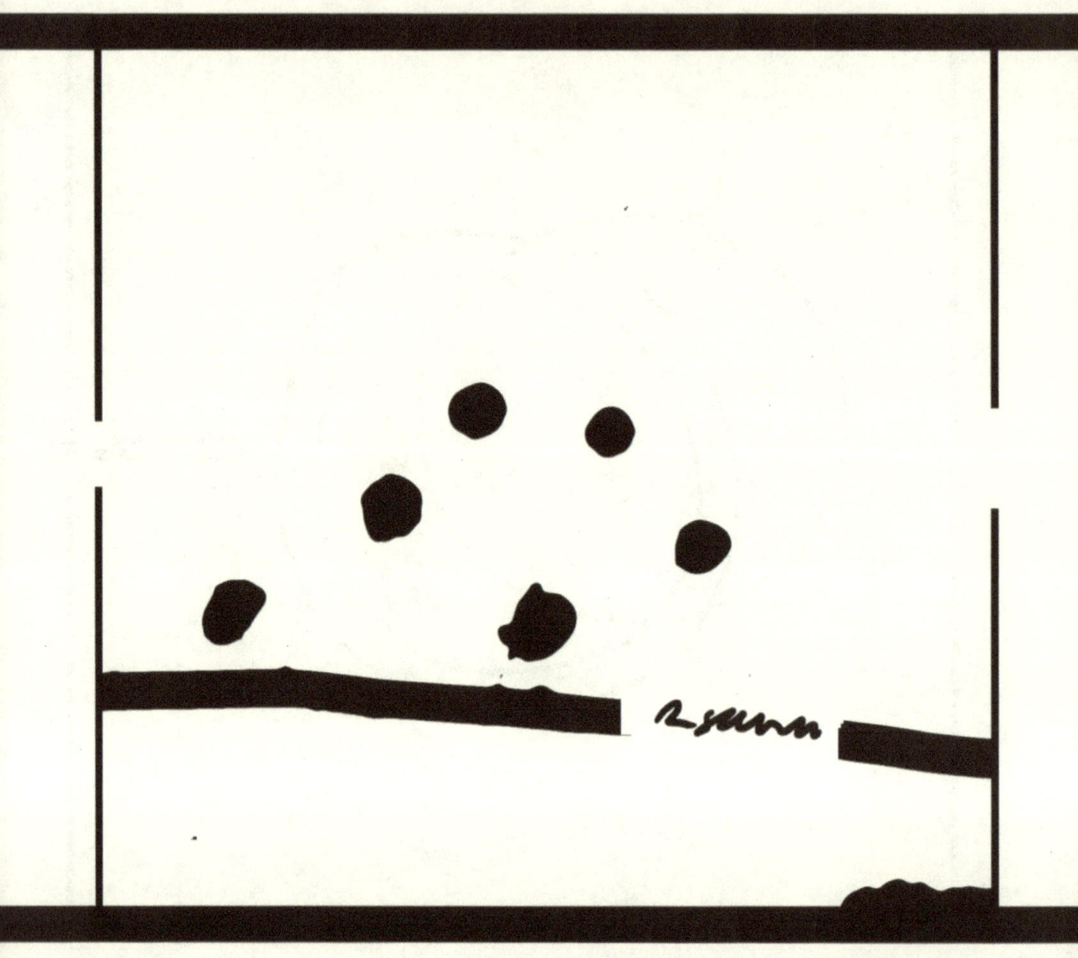

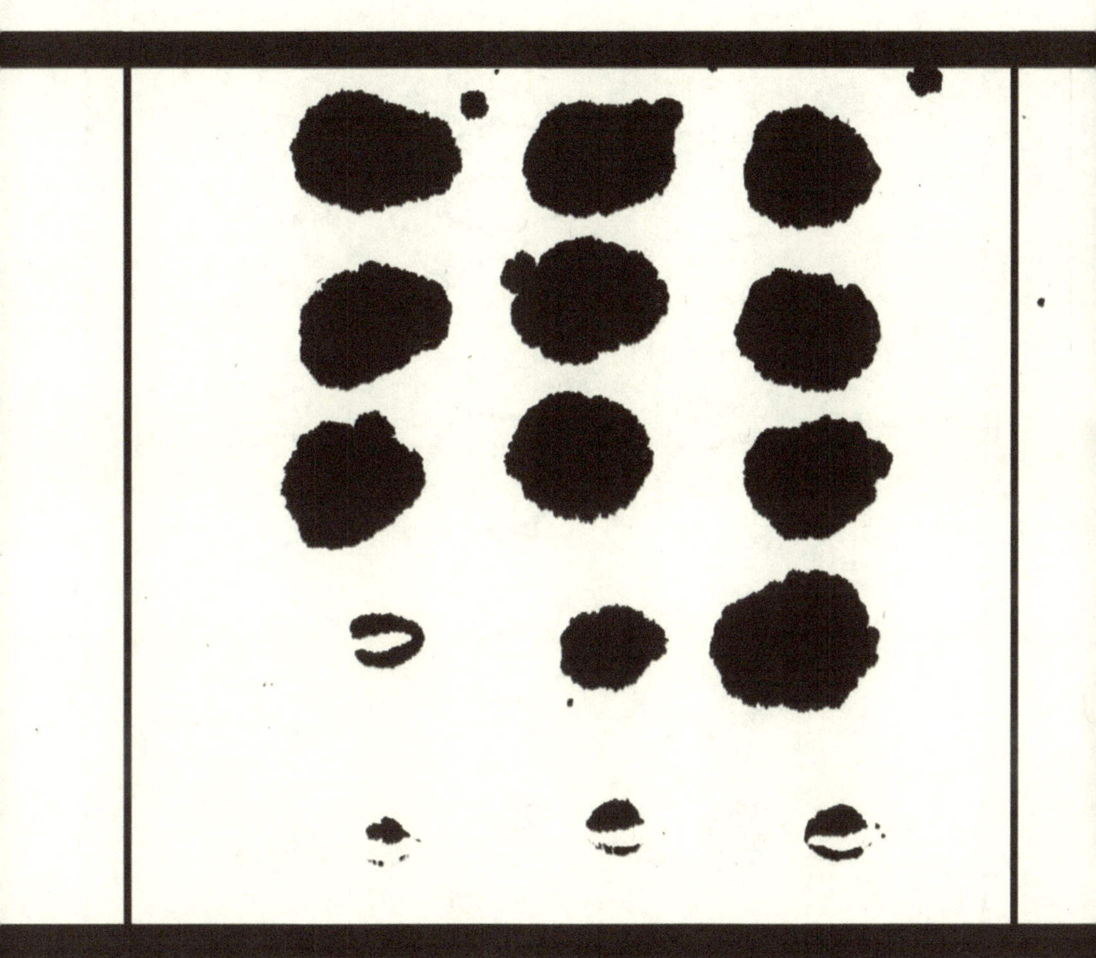

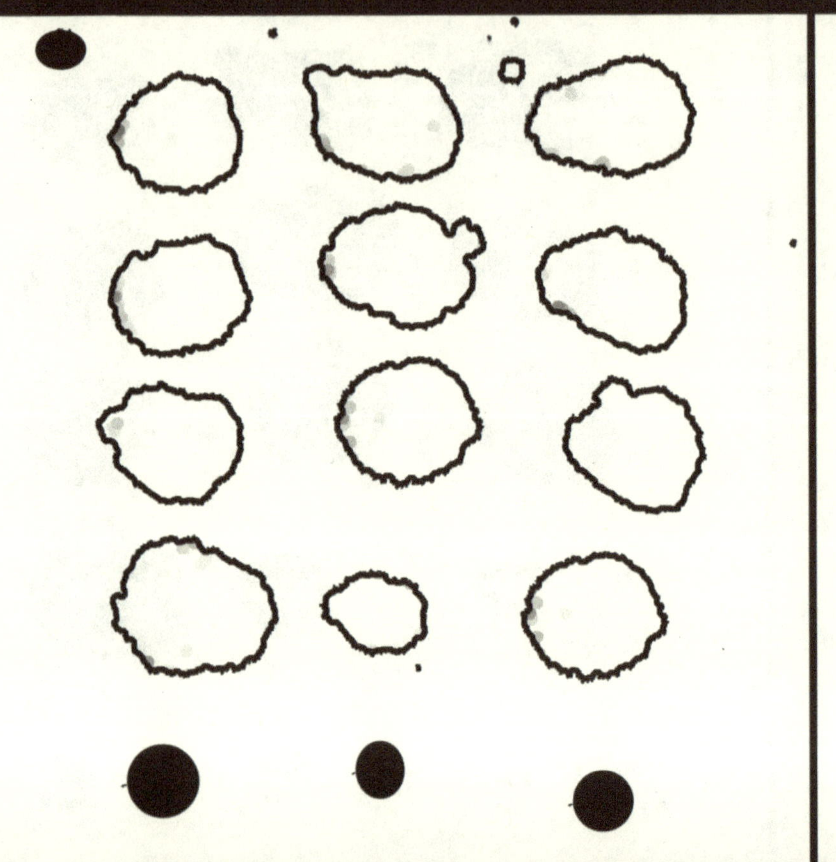

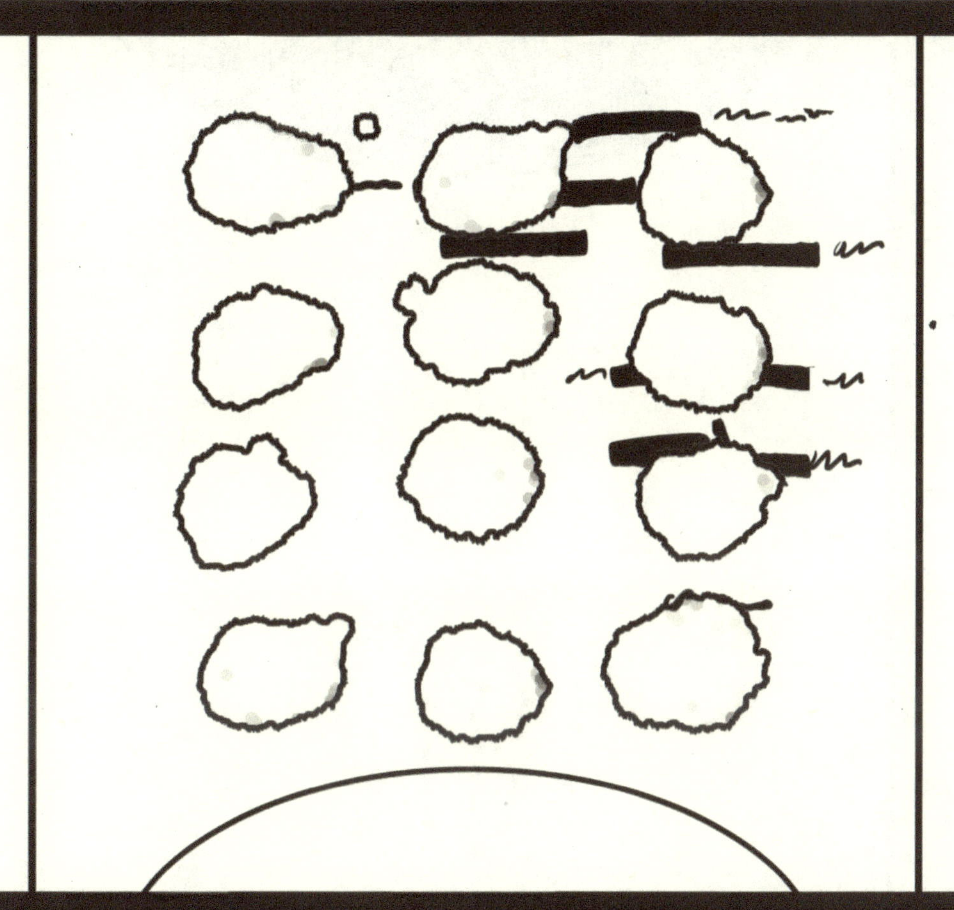

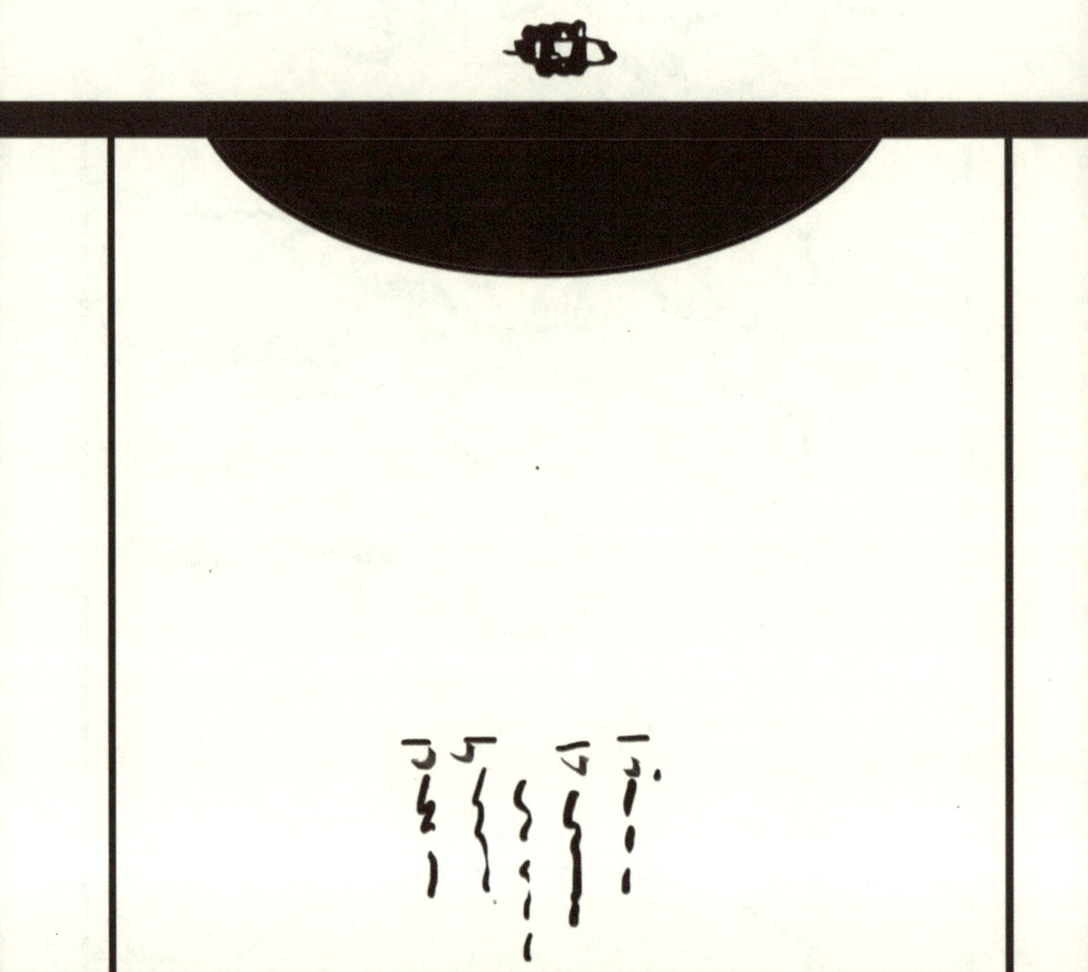

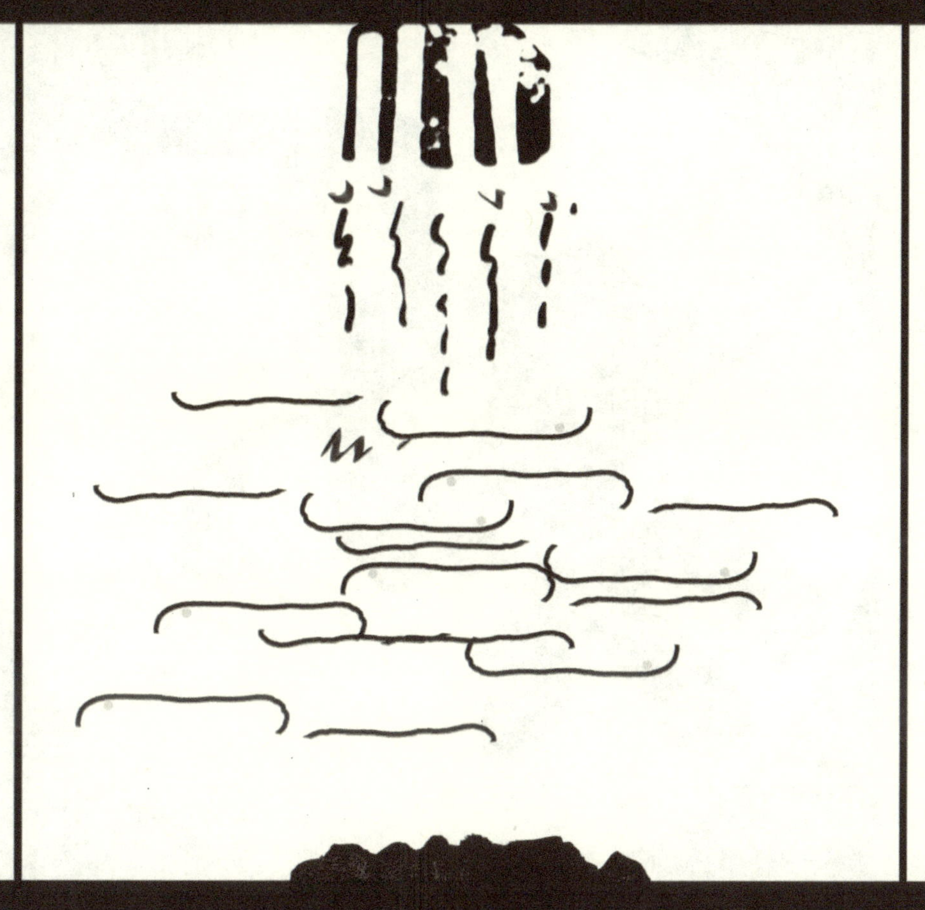

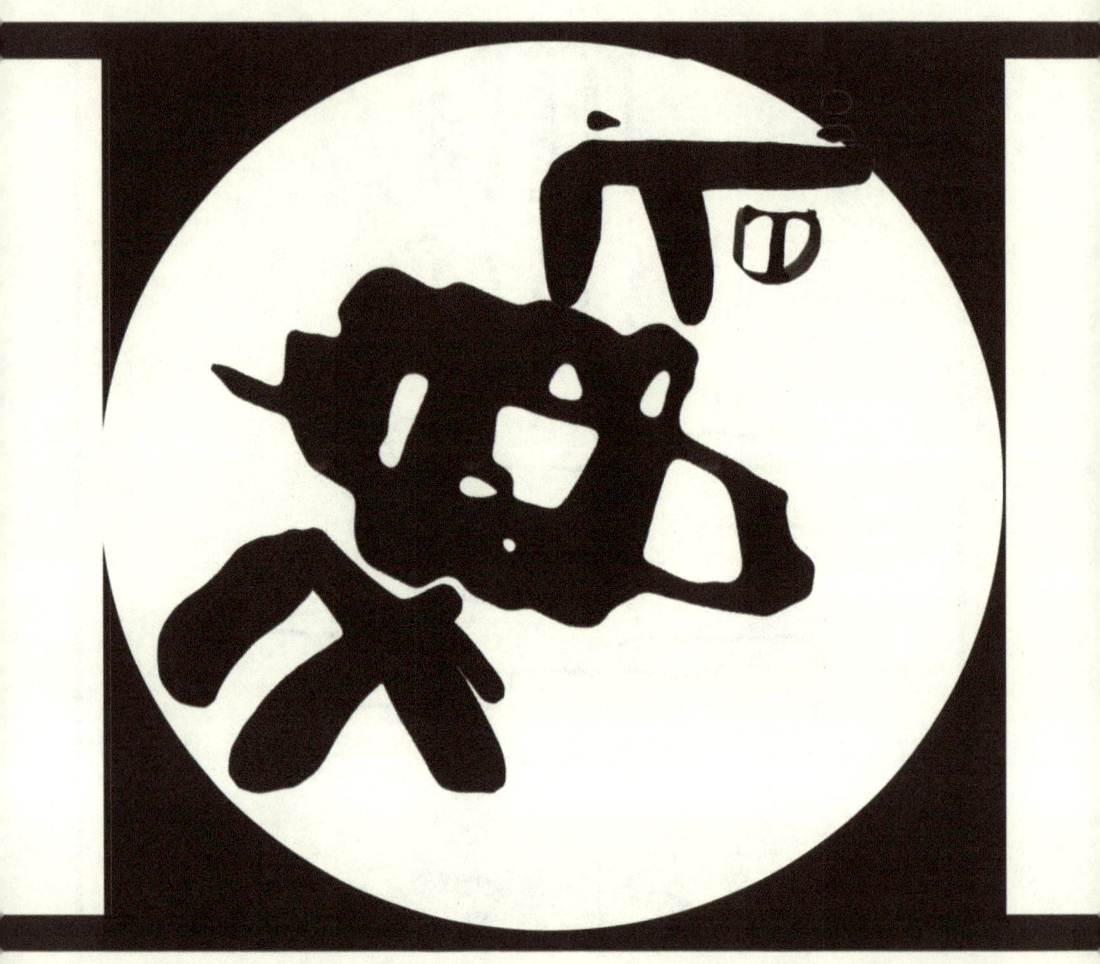

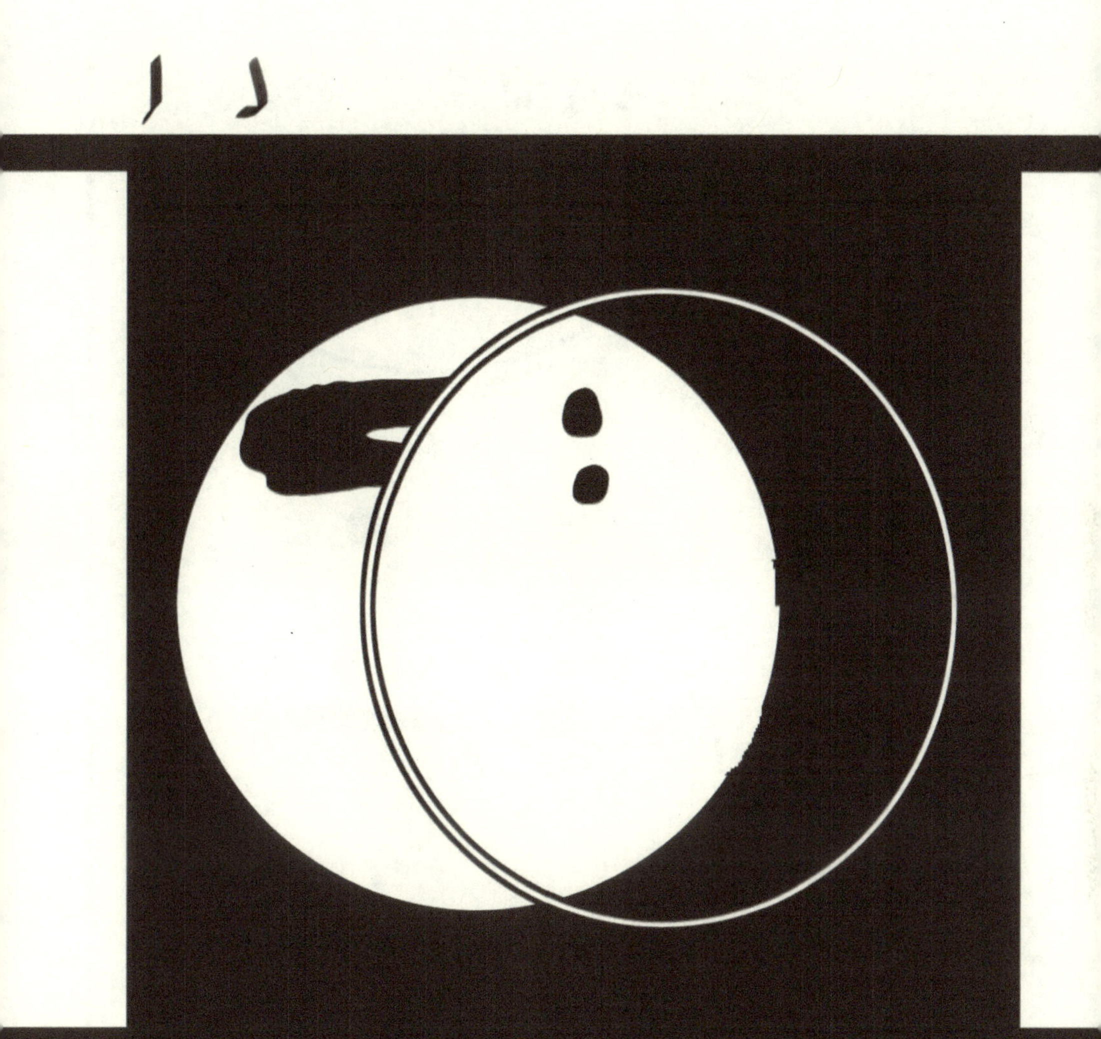

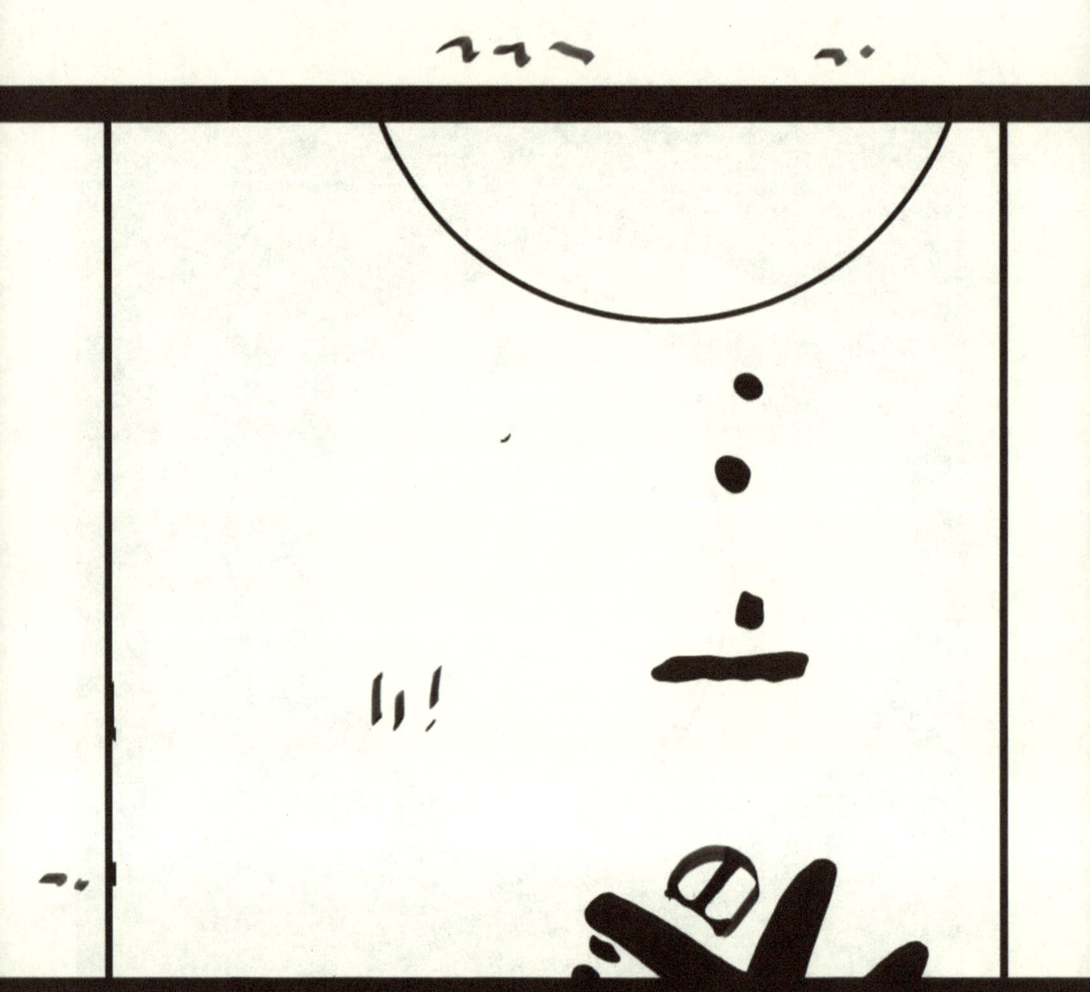

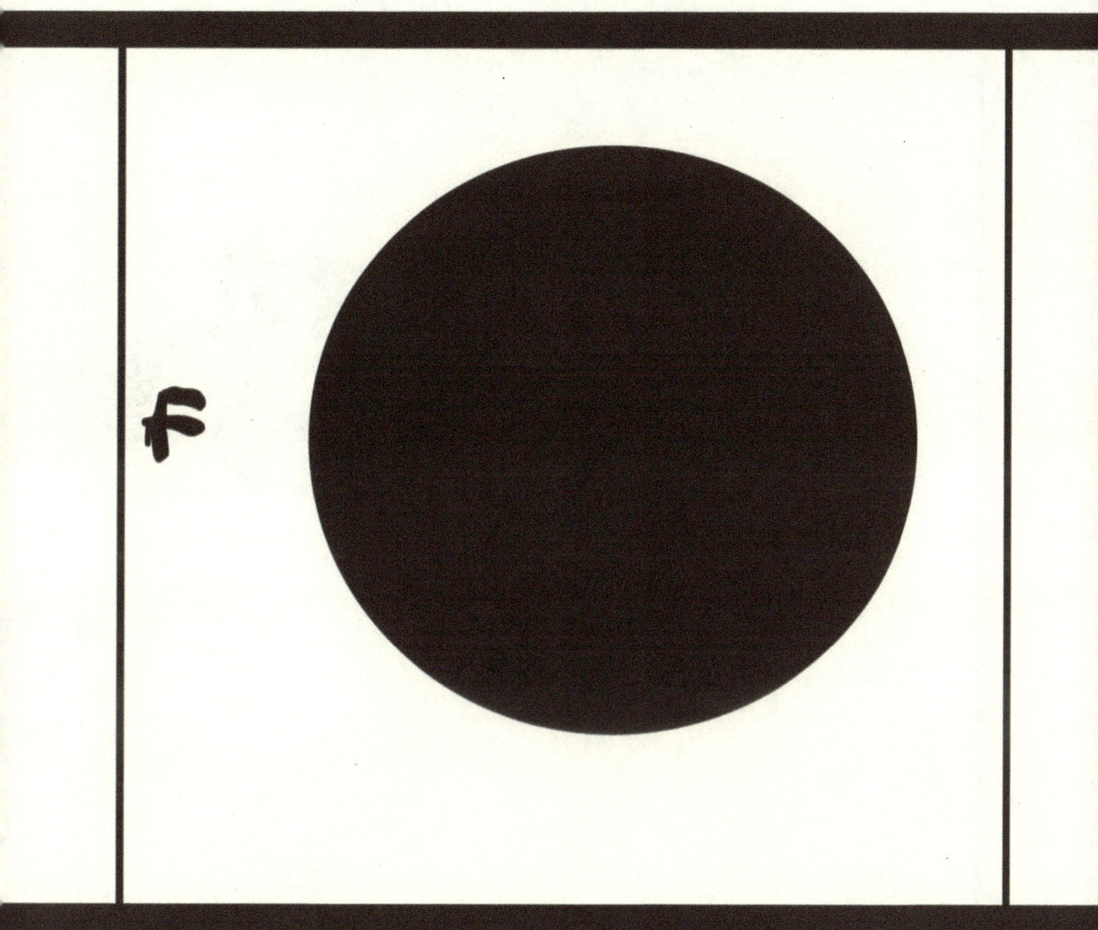
F

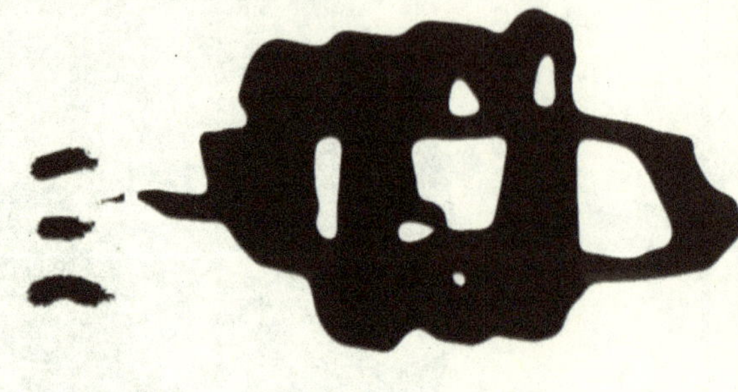

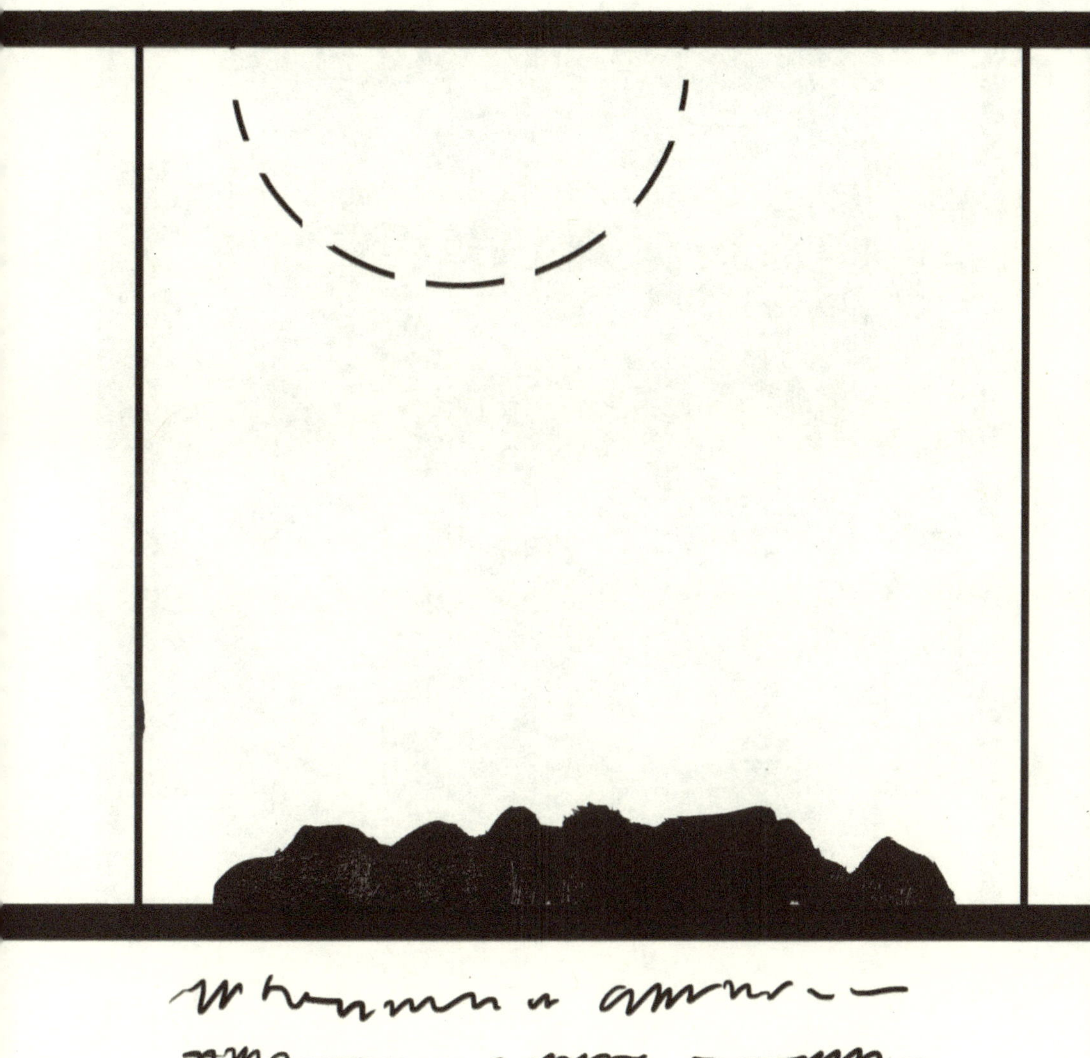

zinc zanc zunc

an asemic conjugation

Conjugation indicates that zinc is a verb, which it isn't. But here, apparently it is. *Zinc* as a particular sound bite is derived from the German, 'zinc', which may in turn come from the Persian word 'sing', meaning s t o n e.

As a verb what is zinc's function? If it's symbolic what is its anchor? When active, can it be followed? Can it be traced through our time zones? Zinc can be visible, as well as elusive.

The verb *zinc*, relieved of solid, metalic and elemental responsibilities, is free. Freedom is, ostensibly, desirable - it is frequently a goal. But verbs do not have desires. Zinc is relegated to desireless action, to the scope and scape of its own performances, wherever they may occur.

Rosaire Appel (NYC) is an ex-writer, graphic artist exploring the betweens of reading/looking/listening. She makes books (commercially printed, hand-made and recycled), ink drawings and digital drawings. Her subject is, basically, visual language. Using a combination of abstract comics and asemic writing, she develops sequences which remain open to interpretation by keeping the relationship between the viewer and the work active. Her website is: www.rosaireappel.com.

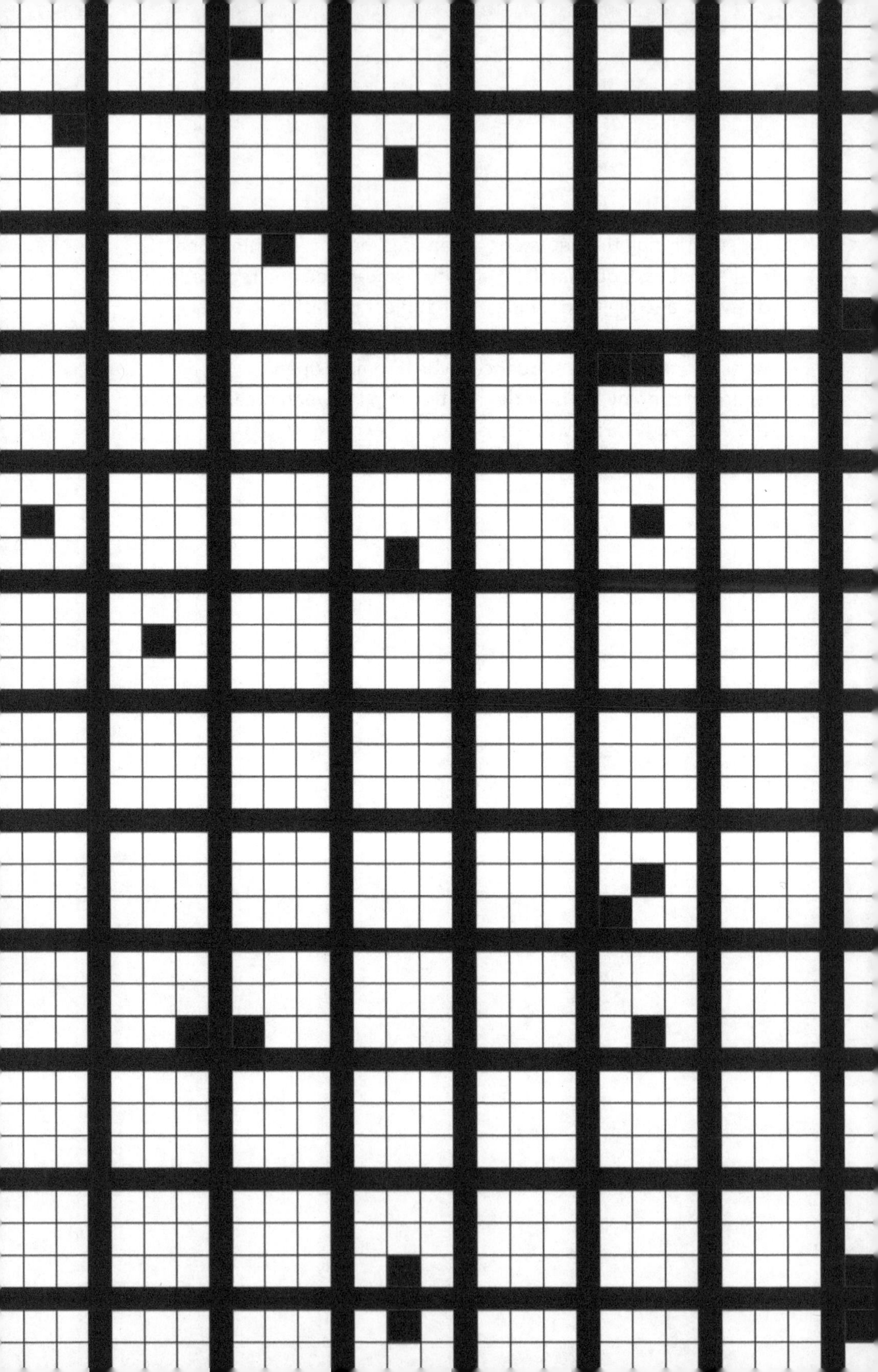

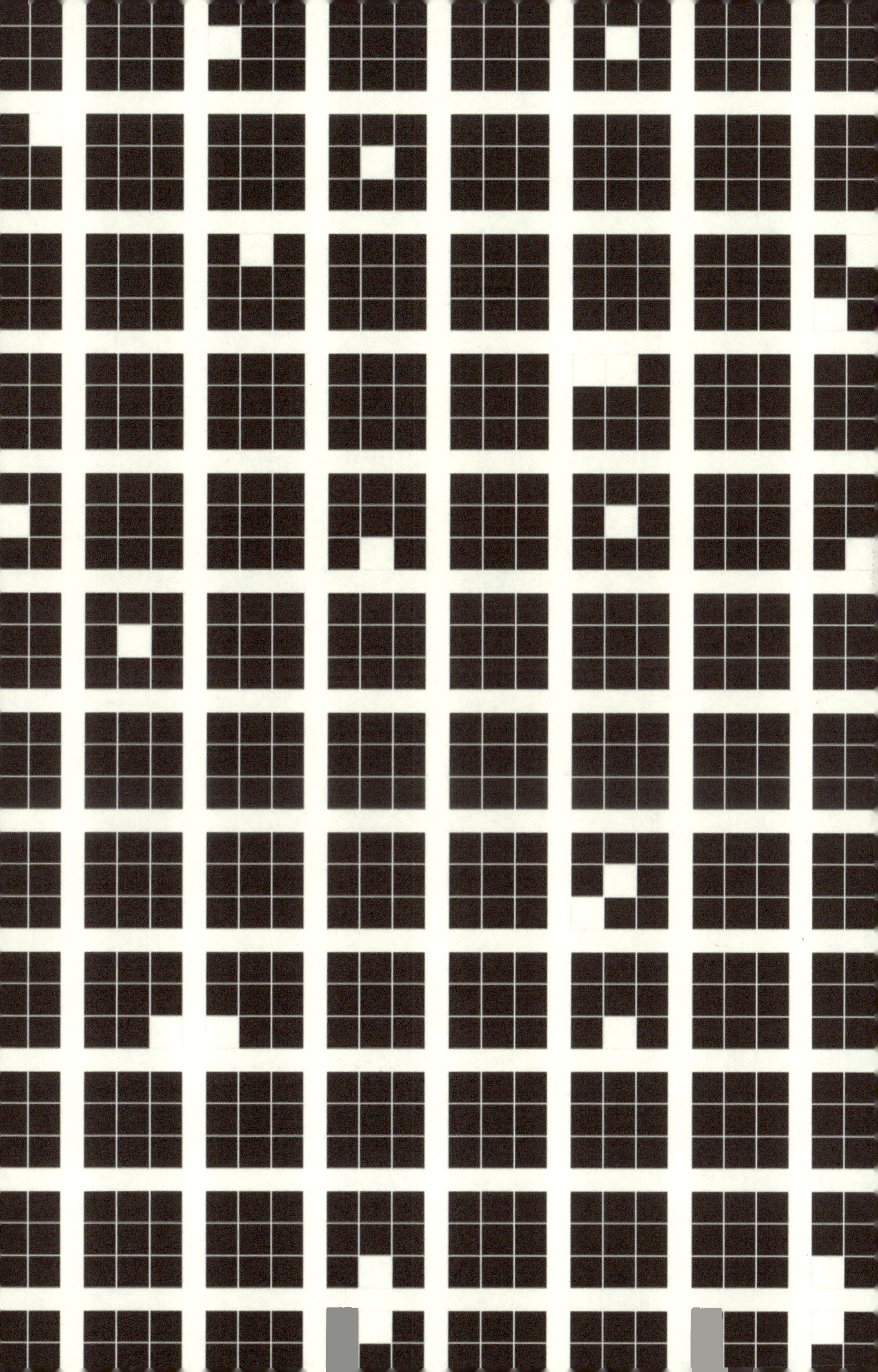

www.ingramcontent.com/pod-product-compliance
Lightning Source LLC
LaVergne TN
LVHW051017080826
845145LV00009B/2666